PRAISE FOR TOM PALMER'S WORLD-WAR FICTION ...

"The best children's fiction book I've yet read about the Holocaust"   **TIM ROBERTSON, CEO OF THE ANNE FRANK TRUST UK, ON** *AFTER THE WAR*

"A moving and thought-provoking read"   **LOUISE STAFFORD, THE NATIONAL HOLOCAUST CENTRE AND MUSEUM, ON** *AFTER THE WAR*

"The book every teacher of the Holocaust needs"   **KATE HEAP, SCOPE FOR THE IMAGINATION, ON** *AFTER THE WAR*

"Devastatingly moving and massively important, and, crucially, fantastically accessible"   ***BOOKS FOR KEEPS* ON** *AFTER THE WAR*

"[Palmer's] most compelling bit of real-life hidden history yet" **THE LETTERPRESS PROJECT ON** *AFTER THE WAR*

"A touching, concisely told yet never dumbed-down story of childhood during wartime. If you are new to his books, then prepare to be astounded"   ***BOOKS FOR TOPICS* ON** *AFTER THE WAR*

"Historical fiction doesn't get much better than this" **LOVEREADING4KIDS ON** *ARCTIC STAR*

"I'm awestruck by his ability to make history come alive and resonate emotionally in beautifully compact prose ... Palmer's writing is sharp like a chisel, finding the heart under the harsh cold of war"   **CHRIS SOUL ON** *ARCTIC STAR*

"Fantastic writing with a wide-ranging narrative, this story will prompt all who read it to think differe
NATIONAL LITERACY TRUST ON *D-DAY D(*

"Tom Palmer is, to my mind, the best author writing accessible history-inspired children's fiction today" **NORTH OF SCOTLAND NEWSPAPERS ON** *D-DAY DOG*

"Such an important book ... Brilliantly researched, full of fascinating facts which are woven together to create a truly moving and gripping read" **BOOKS FOR TOPICS ON** *D-DAY DOG*

"A true tribute to soldiers, civilians and animals caught up in conflict" **ARMADILLO MAGAZINE ON** *D-DAY DOG*

"Tom Palmer has created a poignant story with different voices which manages deftly to explore painful memories of the war while keeping a foot firmly in the present" **JUST IMAGINE ON** *ARMISTICE RUNNER*

"Today and yesterday are seamlessly woven together ... will move readers in lots of different ways" **LOVEREADING4KIDS ON** *ARMISTICE RUNNER*

"Without doubt one of the finest war books I have read in a long time" **THE READING ZONE ON** *ARMISTICE RUNNER*

"Powerfully poignant ... not to be missed" **SCOTT EVANS, THE READER TEACHER, ON** *ARMISTICE RUNNER*

"It's a stroke of brilliance to pair football with wartime history, and this combination is sure to enthral readers ... a lesson in empathy as much as history" **BOOKTRUST ON** *OVER THE LINE*

"Another text that marks [Palmer] out as a writer determined to find the soul within the soldier ... its fast pace will keep readers hurtling through" **JUST IMAGINE ON** *OVER THE LINE*

RESIST

RESIST

TOM PALMER

Barrington Stoke

First published in 2022 in Great Britain by
Barrington Stoke Ltd
18 Walker Street, Edinburgh, EH3 7LP

www.barringtonstoke.co.uk

Text © 2022 Tom Palmer
Illustration © 2022 Tom Clohosy Cole

A CIP catalogue record for this book is available
from the British Library upon request

ISBN: 978-1-80090-106-3

Printed and bound by CPI Group (UK) Ltd, Croydon, CR0 4YY

For Ailsa Bathgate,
with huge gratitude

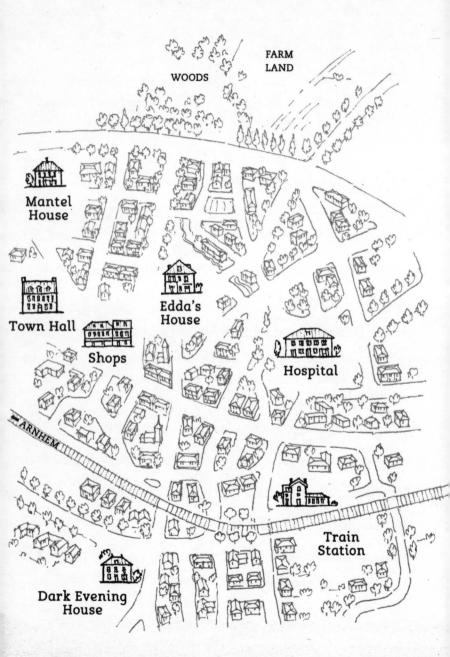

VELP, 1943

WOODS

FARM LAND

Mantel House

Town Hall

Shops

Edda's House

Hospital

ARNHEM

Train Station

Dark Evening House

Map illustration © James Innerdale

ONE

Velp, the Netherlands, 1943 – under occupation

Edda didn't have time to change direction before the level-crossing barrier came down. The barrier blocked the road that ran over the railway track to the side of the station. With a train about to leave, she was forced to stop along with a dozen other cyclists.

A pair of German soldiers manning the checkpoint ran their eyes over Edda and the others. Edda didn't dare to look at them. If they saw the fear on her face, they would be suspicious – they might guess what she was doing.

But Edda knew she could not just turn and cycle away. That would also draw their attention. She had to wait and behave as if she was just an ordinary teenager cycling home from school.

It was fortunate for Edda that there were other cyclists being held up at the barrier. It helped her to blend in. The Germans had been occupying the Netherlands for over three years now, and because they had taken almost all the country's petrol, most people travelled by bicycle. But as the Germans had also taken most of the rubber needed for inner tubes, those cyclists had to stuff their tyres with straw, while others had even made wooden wheels for their bikes.

The Nazis took everything, Edda thought. You couldn't do anything or go anywhere without being reminded that they were here.

But the state of her bicycle tyres was the least of Edda's problems.

The real worry was what she was carrying. A sheaf of illegal resistance newsletters that she was to deliver to addresses south of the railway line. Sheets printed with details about the latest anti-German resistance activity – attacks on Nazi soldiers or troop trains, for example – as the Dutch people tried to fight back against their occupiers.

If the Nazi guards at the checkpoint found the newsletters, they'd torture Edda to find out where she had got them from, then they'd kill her. No doubt about that.

Edda could feel sweat on her forehead even though it was a cool evening. Eyes still fixed ahead, she tried to look calm as she remembered the words of the man who had handed her the newsletters to deliver.

"Avoid the Nazis if you can," he'd said. "If you think they're going to stop you, throw the

newsletters away. If that's not possible, act like an innocent child so they don't search you."

Edda had no chance of throwing anything away now she was just a few metres from the German soldiers, and her heart raced ever faster as she saw that one of them had started to check each cyclist's ID card.

All people living in the Netherlands aged fourteen and over had to carry an ID card bearing their photograph, fingerprints and other personal details. Edda now fished hers out of her bag, her mind a frenzy of panicked questions. What if they searched her? What if they found the newsletters?

She glanced at the card in her hand, feeling the usual jolt at seeing the name there – Edda. Not her real name, which was Audrey. But when she had returned to the Netherlands from school in England nearly four years earlier, her mother had banned

her from using Audrey. It was an English name and identified her as British, like her father. That alone would make the Germans suspicious of her and perhaps more curious about what she was carrying.

As she waited for her turn, Edda closed her eyes and tried to remember why on earth she had agreed to take on this dangerous task. The fear she felt now was too much to bear. But she knew she only had herself to blame.

Edda had heard about the work of the Dutch resistance and wanted to get involved – to do more than just wash bandages and serve food to patients in the hospital where she volunteered after school. And she knew that the doctor there, Dr Hendrik Visser 't Hooft, was an important figure in the resistance.

When she'd approached him, Dr Visser 't Hooft was unsure about her offer of help. Edda was just

a young girl. "Do you really want to get involved in such dangerous work?" he asked.

But Edda was determined, so Dr Visser 't Hooft gave her a test. He asked her to memorise five addresses, which she did easily. So then he challenged her to remember ten.

Again, this was easy for Edda.

"You have a fine memory," he commented.

"It's from ballet," Edda told him. "We have to remember dozens of positions and moves. We have to have good memories."

The doctor smiled. "Then I have the perfect job for you," he said. "I would like you to deliver resistance newsletters to multiple addresses if you can?"

Edda scowled now at that memory, still waiting for the train to leave and the barrier to rise. She had been so naive to imagine she could do this. More than naive. She had been stupid.

Boasting about how she had a good memory because of her dance classes.

Seriously?

A soldier stopped in front of her. His gloved hand on her handlebars made Edda want to push him away.

"ID?" he demanded.

Edda handed the card to him and he checked it, squinting at the photograph. Then he glanced at her bag.

"Bag. Open."

Edda felt like she might be sick, but she had no choice other than to lift her satchel off her shoulder. She handed it to the soldier and looked down the platform, trying to distract herself from the fear that made her feel like she might collapse.

She could see more German soldiers forcing people onto a train. The people looked familiar. They

were local. She recognised some. They had suitcases. The children seemed to be crying. Edda realised that some of the adults were crying too. But she was too scared for herself at that moment to think clearly about what was happening on the platform.

"What is this?" the soldier asked, lifting some sheets of paper out of her bag.

Edda turned back to face the soldier and looked him in the eye, trying to pretend she had nothing to hide.

"School work." She could hear her voice wavering.

After a few moments, the soldier handed the sheets back, then moved on to the next person.

Edda took in a fast deep breath, then slowly exhaled, relieved that she had decided not to carry the illegal newsletters in her bag.

Trembling, she looked again at the train, seeing

the distressed faces of the passengers staring back at her.

Where were these people being taken? She had heard the rumours. Some were transported to Germany as slave labour – mainly young Dutch men over the age of eighteen. But others were taken to huge camps where many of them were murdered. Could it be true?

Edda shuddered. She hated the Nazis – hated what they had done to the Netherlands and to people that she loved. To her family.

Her older brother, Alex, had been forced into hiding. And she could hardly bear to think about what had happened to her uncle Otto ...

No, this wasn't the time to think about these things. She had to stay sharp. She had to make a choice. Now. And it was a difficult one.

When the barrier lifted, would she give up

this madness of delivering newsletters and just go home where she would be safe? Or could she find the courage to carry on and deliver them, even if it meant putting herself through more of this almost unbearable fear?

TWO

Her heart pounding now the barrier had been raised, Edda cycled over the railway tracks and past half a dozen German soldiers on the other side.

She heard laughter and realised that the soldiers were mocking the people staring helplessly from the train.

Now anger overwhelmed Edda. She couldn't do anything to stop these disgusting men laughing, or to help the people who had been forced onto the train. But she could spread news of the resistance, pass the story on.

Cycling hard, Edda found the street she had been

asked to visit and hid her bicycle within a large bush.

A chilly breeze ruffled the bush as she did so, causing the leaves to tremble. Sitting on the pavement, but hidden by the foliage, Edda removed the newsletters that she had stuffed down the side of her oversized wool socks.

Her mind was made up. She would find the courage she needed.

There was no one about as Edda moved stealthily through the front gardens of the houses she was to deliver to. She slipped between rosebushes and leaped over vegetable patches in which people grew their own potatoes and greens to make up for the food shortages.

This ability to leap and run and land without making a sound was another skill she had learned from dance – like her good memory. It all proved so useful tonight as she dropped off the newsletters and slipped away unnoticed.

It took her just a few minutes to deliver to all the houses that she had been asked to visit. Her first mission for the resistance was complete.

Now she had to get home.

Edda cycled back to the station, cautiously checking from a distance to see if the barrier at the level crossing was down. She didn't want to be stopped again and attract the attention of the soldiers by returning so quickly.

The moon had come out now, and a flood of light illuminated the streets and the station. Yes. The barrier was down again. It was not safe to approach the crossing. Not yet.

Edda found a small cluster of trees, laid her bicycle on the grass and sat down. With the light of the moon so bright, she took the opportunity to glance at the spare copy of the newsletter she had kept for herself.

The newsletter was called *De Oranjekrant*. It was small, the size of a children's comic, just two sheets thick. After reading about how the resistance were raising money to help find safe houses for Jewish people to escape the Nazis, Edda's attention was drawn to a list of those the newsletter said were "not to be trusted".

Edda had heard about people like this. She remembered older children at school calling them "Nazi sympathisers" or "collaborators" and talking disgustedly about these local people who were helping the Germans. And here they were, listed for everyone to see.

Edda ran her finger down the list, hoping that none of her friends' parents or adults she knew from school or dance were there. Then her finger stopped at a familiar name.

She dropped the newsletter in horror. Because

the name she had seen printed there in black and white was Ella van Heemstra.

Ella van Heemstra was Edda's mother.

THREE

After returning home that night, Edda barely slept, unable to stop thinking about her mother's name printed in *De Oranjekrant*. She was distracted throughout the next day at school, and it was still on her mind when she arrived at the hospital to volunteer.

Today, she would be washing bandages again. Before the war, bandages would only be used once and thrown away or burned after they had been lifted off wounds, stained with blood. Now, with supplies dwindling, the bandages needed to be recycled. They had to be boiled to sterilise them.

Using a pair of wooden tongs to dip them deep into the boiling water, Edda would then stretch them out to dry before rolling them up for reuse.

Alone in the laundry room, Edda had peace to think as she worked. Although she had been so shocked to see her mum's name in *De Oranjekrant*, Edda knew that there had to be a reason it was there. But what?

Edda went over the things her mum did, the people she knew, the life she had lived. And then it came to her. A photograph that used to sit on the sideboard in their flat in Arnhem a couple of years ago. It was a picture of her mum with some friends in Munich in Germany before the war, and Edda remembered her mum telling her that it had been taken on the day that she'd met Hitler.

Adolf Hitler.

So was it true then? Was her mum a Nazi sympathiser, not to be trusted?

When they had moved to live with Opa, Edda's grandad, here in Velp, the photograph had disappeared. Edda wondered where it had gone and why she had never asked Mum about it in the first place. How had it come about that Mum had met that dreadful man?

"Edda? How are you today?"

Edda jumped. The voice shocked her out of her troubled thoughts. She turned to see Dr Visser 't Hooft. He was tall and athletic. It was only a few years since he had won an Olympic silver medal as part of the Dutch field-hockey team, making him something of a local celebrity.

"Good, thank you," Edda replied, flustered by his sudden arrival.

"I'm sorry," he said. "I startled you."

Edda shook her head. "It's fine. I was miles away."

The doctor glanced back through the door and

lowered his voice. "And your trip yesterday. Did it go well?"

"I got caught on the wrong side of the railway track for a while and had to wait for the train to pass," she began to explain, but then decided she'd said enough. Edda knew that she should keep things simple.

She also knew that she didn't want to do it again. That it had been too frightening. But she couldn't find the right words to tell him this.

"That must have been difficult." Dr Visser 't Hooft looked concerned. "Are you OK now?"

"Yes. I am. Now."

"You're sure?"

"I'm sure," Edda replied, looking directly at the doctor. She knew that this was her chance to back out, to tell him that she was too scared to take on any more work like that, but something made her keep quiet.

The doctor watched Edda at her work for a few moments, then changed the subject.

"You like to dance, Edda," he said. "Is that right?"

Edda stopped working and turned to study the doctor. She could feel that a huge grin had broken out on her face. Dance was her favourite subject, her favourite thing altogether. She had been learning since she was a small child, something her mum had always encouraged. She had attended lessons every week, sometimes performed in shows. Her teacher had told her that she had great talent, that if she worked hard, she had a future on the stage.

"I do," she enthused.

"I remember you telling me," Dr Visser 't Hooft said. "And since then I have heard from friends about some of the dance recitals that you've taken part in. I understand you were one of the stars of the show. Is that right?"

Yes. It was right. Edda had been the star, given the best solos by her teacher, and had loved every minute of being so good at something she enjoyed. But Edda remembered what her mum had always said: *Be modest. Don't boast. Just say thank you.*

"Not really," Edda answered. "No, but ... I ... I love to dance."

The doctor nodded, then looked down the corridor again.

"Colleagues who work here at the hospital are planning an evening of entertainment," he told her. "To help some of the more unfortunate people in the Netherlands. People in hiding. I think you understand what I mean."

Edda understood. The image of the people being forced onto the train the night before was burned into her memory. She had read about these fundraising efforts in the newsletter only last night.

Money was needed to help move people to safety, to keep them hidden from the Nazis.

Those people in hiding were known as *onderduikers* and included Jews and others deemed "undesirable" by the Nazis, as well as young men who wanted to avoid being forced to fight in the German army. Young men like Edda's brother Alex.

"We call these 'dark evenings'," Dr Visser 't Hooft said. "We want to put on a performance. Music, dance, readings. To entertain our friends in Velp and to raise money. It would be a secret performance. After dark."

Edda felt excitement rush through her body.

"And," Dr Visser 't Hooft went on, "I would like you to ask your mother if you could possibly dance for us. She would need to come too, of course."

Edda felt another burst of excitement. Then a realisation.

Surely this meant that Dr Visser 't Hooft thought Mum was OK, that she could be trusted? Why would Mum be invited to a secret resistance fundraising show if they suspected her of being a Nazi sympathiser? This must be a good thing? Edda felt confused, but her longing to dance made her put all her worries about her mum to one side.

"I would love to," she said.

"But you must ask your mother," Dr Visser 't Hooft said. "It is her decision."

"Yes, yes." Edda knew she was still grinning. "But she will say yes. I know she will."

FOUR

"No."

Edda couldn't believe what she was hearing. They had only just sat down to eat at the dining table and now she was standing again in disbelief, watched by her mum, Opa, brother Ian and Aunt Miesje.

Edda had asked the question: "Can I dance at Dr Visser 't Hooft's fundraising evening?"

Her mum was still shaking her head.

Edda wanted to leave the table and run to her room. She stared at her mum, who looked elegant as ever in her jacket and blouse, a string of pearls, bright red lipstick and not a hair out of place.

Edda rarely argued with her mum. And she didn't want to upset her aunt, who was twisting her napkin, eyes down, anxious. The rule at home was always no disagreements in front of Miesje. Aunt Miesje needed protecting since the events that had led to the death of Uncle Otto.

"Sit down, Edda," Mum said calmly.

Edda sat and saw her brother looking at Mum, ready to challenge her. Ian was three years older than Edda and four years younger than their older brother, Alex. He was as tall as Mum already and had a messy blond flop of hair. He looked interested, even impressed, that Edda had been asked to take part.

"Let her do it, Mum," Ian said. "Please."

Mum shook her head, glancing at Aunt Miesje, then back at Ian.

"You love to see her dance," Ian persisted.

Mum finished chewing and nodded. "I do," she said. "There is nothing in the world I love more than seeing Edda dance."

"Then let her do it," Ian pressed.

"No."

"Why not?"

Ian wasn't going to let this go. Edda had to try hard not to smile. It was exciting to see someone standing up to Mum.

"Because it is dangerous, Ian," Mum explained. "Because it is illegal. Because it is a risk. To Edda. And to us all. We must be careful."

Ian was shaking his head. "We must do what the Germans tell us?" he snorted. "We must never be seen to be going against what the Germans wish for us?"

"Ian." Opa's voice cracked like a gunshot. "Don't speak to your mother like that."

Ian leaned back in his chair and glanced helplessly at Edda. "I'm sorry, sir," he said to Opa.

"And your mother," Opa added. "Apologise to her too."

"I'm sorry, Mum."

Edda hated adults sometimes. Telling you what could happen and what couldn't. Making all the decisions. Making her miserable. But she had tried, and Ian had tried, and now Opa was backing Mum – so that would be that.

They ate in an uncomfortable silence. A potato broth with the tiniest bits of meat floating around in it. Ration food. Edda couldn't remember the last time she'd chewed on a proper-sized piece of meat. But at least there were potatoes. The Germans hadn't taken all of them yet.

Spooning her soup in silence, Edda noted that Mum and Aunt Miesje had set the table like they

always did. Tablecloth. The best cutlery. Napkins.
Placemats. A drinking glass each. All for a bowl of
potato soup.

The table made her angry. Her mum was so
concerned about keeping up appearances when the
world around them was in chaos. And Edda was
eager for things to be angry about now. She wanted
to go to her room, grab the resistance newsletter
and slam it down in front of her mum.

Here. Read what they think about you! she
might shout.

But she wouldn't. All that would stay in her
head. She certainly wouldn't say a word when Aunt
Miesje was there.

Edda glanced at the empty chair next to
her aunt. She really struggled with that chair. It
symbolised the gloom that filled the house the five
of them shared. Until not so long ago, that chair had

been occupied by Uncle Otto, Aunt Miesje's husband. But not any more.

The memories were unavoidable now. It had happened earlier in the occupation. The Nazis invaded the Netherlands in May 1940, and at first they had been friendly, even courteous, occupiers.

But that did not last long.

Soon the Nazis began to pick on the Jewish people in the Netherlands. Resistance to the occupation grew. Men and women joined together secretly to make trouble for the occupiers. They would tear down German signposts, even blow up trains.

The Germans hit back against these attacks by taking four hundred and sixty men hostage. Important men from across the Netherlands. They called them "death candidates". The idea was that every time the resistance acted against the Germans, some of the death candidates would be shot. Executed.

One of the men taken hostage was Uncle Otto. And later that summer, when the resistance attacked another train, the Germans said they would execute some of the death candidates.

No one thought they would go through with it. But they did.

No one imagined Uncle Otto would be one of the first five to be executed. But they were wrong. Uncle Otto was taken with four other men into some woods and shot.

The shock and grief caused by his execution had been devastating. A year later later, the family was still reeling.

As usually happened when the mood around the dining table dipped, Opa filled the uncomfortable silence. Sometimes he tried to make them laugh. Other times he told them stories from his youth. Stories they had heard before but still enjoyed.

And sometimes he commented on the occupation.

"I handed our radio in this afternoon," he said gravely.

"Filthy *moffen*," Ian said under his breath.

"Ian!" Mum scolded, disapproving of the rude word used for the Germans.

"Well, how are we to know what's happening in the war without a radio?" Ian asked. "How will we know if the Allies are going to come and liberate us? Or how badly the Germans are doing in Russia?"

The family had been listening to an illegal radio programme called *Radio Oranje* since the Germans had invaded. It was broadcast by the BBC from Britain and kept them up to date with news about how the war was going. Sometimes there were messages from the Queen of the Netherlands, who had escaped to England – messages encouraging the Dutch people to resist the Nazis.

If you were caught listening to *Radio Oranje*, you would be punished. But people still tuned in anyway. That was why the Nazis were confiscating everyone's radios.

"We should have hidden ours," Ian said.

Opa shook his head. "No. You have to register to own a radio, so a list of owners is kept at the town hall. The Germans now have that list. So they knew we had a radio."

Edda watched Mum shiver.

"But Mantel has a radio that the Germans don't know about," Opa went on. "He used to buy and sell them. We shall have to visit him one night. After dark. What do you think, Edda? Would you come with me? It'd be like a secret mission."

"Yes," Edda said firmly, taking care not to look at her mum.

FIVE

One week after handing the family radio in to the
Nazis, Opa asked Ian and Edda to join him for a
walk. It was 8.30 p.m., after the 8 p.m. curfew set by
the enemy, meaning people were not allowed out of
their houses.

"Where are you going?" Mum complained.

"A walk. Two children and their grandfather.
And that's all I can tell you," Opa said, grinning
secretively.

Mum rolled her eyes.

It was dark outside apart from German
searchlights criss-crossing the sky. There was

nobody about. Nobody at all. It reminded Edda of the night walks her two brothers would take her on before the war broke out, searching the woods and fields for wild animals and the skies for shooting stars.

But it was different tonight. It was so completely quiet, frighteningly quiet. No people. No vehicles. No wind to make sounds in the trees or whistle round the eaves of the buildings. All the windows of the houses were dark, people hidden inside trying to keep out of the way of the occupying Germans.

Edda felt like all her senses had been supercharged. She thought she heard the click of a lock on the inside of a door across the street, an aeroplane buzzing thousands of metres up in the sky.

It was hard not to scan the skies for Allied aeroplanes once she thought she had heard one. Edda knew that the British and Americans flew high

over the Netherlands night and day to bomb German cities. She imagined them looking down into the darkness now, searching for any source of light that could help them navigate.

But that would be difficult. It was compulsory for Dutch householders to black out their windows with paper covered in tar, stretched over a wooden frame. The streetlights were also turned off to make sure that the Allies were kept in the dark, literally.

They walked without speaking or even whispering. Ian knew the way as they moved down narrow alleyways and around the backs of gardens, avoiding main roads. Opa seemed to be struggling in the dark, so Edda offered him her arm and he took it. She found it easy to pick her way as she marvelled at the thousands of stars above them, brighter than she had seen them before.

As Edda helped Opa, she reflected on how it was

unusual to be touching him. Her grandfather was not a big hugger. He always stood at arm's length when family gatherings began, preferring to take people's coats or offer them a drink than to be involved in displays of affection. But the way he squeezed her arm as they walked in the dark felt good. Like he needed her.

"This is where Mantel lives," Opa said at last.

Ian led them down the path, and as they approached the door, it was opened by Jan Mantel. After a whispered greeting, Jan checked his watch and glanced past them into the dark lane. "It is nearly time for the broadcast," he said. "But someone must be on lookout. Ian?"

"I will." Edda volunteered before Ian could reply. She was enjoying the night – being outside in the dark – and was keen to show she was just as brave as her brother.

The two old men smiled their thanks, then went with Ian into the house, leaving Edda alone under the dark sky.

Edda took a deep breath and opened up her senses to the night. If the Germans came, she would see and hear and even smell them coming. There was no way the three men inside were going to be caught listening to the radio on her watch.

*

Half an hour later, the moon was out as they made their way home from Jan Mantel's. Again, they walked in silence. But this time Edda was at the front, allowing Ian to take Opa's arm. As Opa predicted, they didn't meet another soul, let alone a German patrol or vehicle.

When they arrived, Opa thanked Edda and Ian.

"I'll make sure I have you as my lookout on

any other secret missions I might have, Edda," Opa promised.

Ian and Edda sat on the back step outside the house after Opa had gone in to tell Mum and Aunt Miesje the news from the radio broadcast. The sister and brother were hidden from the main road. It wasn't too cold, and they were enjoying being outside for a while rather than trapped indoors for another evening of curfew. In the dark they could see the backs of their neighbours' houses, trees and shrubs.

"You handled yourself well out and about tonight," Ian commented. "It's almost like you've done it before."

Edda hesitated. What was this?

Ian persisted. "I sometimes wonder what you get up to for the doctor at the hospital."

"I wash bandages," Edda said bluntly.

She knew she must say nothing about delivering the newsletters. Resistance work had to be kept secret. You didn't tell anyone anything. Even your brother. It was for their own safety. The less people knew, the better. If someone was caught by the Germans, they could be tortured and forced to give away all their secrets. Edda already regretted bringing up Dr Visser 't Hooft's dark evening in front of the whole family. But Mum had refused anyway, so perhaps it was OK.

"So what did you hear on the radio?" Edda whispered, changing the subject.

"It was good news," Ian said, shifting to sit with his back to the door. "The Germans are being hammered in Russia. They've lost air superiority over Europe. It's going our way. The *moffen* will be gone before we know it."

Edda grinned. "How long will it take?" she asked. "What will happen next?"

Ian stared up at the stars and began to tell her what he thought was coming.

"Now the Americans are getting more involved, they will really help the British and all the other Allies. Together, they will invade. They are already planning it. One night, they'll all come to liberate the Netherlands and the rest of Europe. Then we'll be free. The end is coming, Edda."

Edda felt a thrill run up her back and arms. The idea of the Germans leaving. Of proper food. Of seeing everyone she loved. Of freedom. "How though?" she said. "How will they invade?"

Now Ian began to speak in English, trying to mimic the voice of Winston Churchill, making a speech that sounded a bit like one of the British Prime Minister's they had heard on the radio before it had to be given up.

"They'll come by sea," he said. "In ships and

submarines. Millions of soldiers heading east from London to the Netherlands across the English Channel. Then – as their ships dock – a million more soldiers will jump from aeroplanes. An airborne army. The skies will be black with parachutes."

Edda was laughing as quietly as she could. She loved to see Ian happy and fooling around. And she loved what she was hearing.

"But is that true?" she asked. "Will it really happen?" And now she found she was crying. Just a bit.

Seeing her tears, Ian took Edda's hands in his. "It will," he said in his own voice. "I promise. One day we will be liberated. We have friends all over the world who are planning to help us right now. And when they come, we'll be able to run around the streets at night laughing and shouting. We'll be able to light up our garden and do whatever we want. I promise you."

Ian held up two fingers, displaying a V for victory just as Churchill always did. "You'll see," he said. "One day."

SIX

For several days after their night-time visit to Jan Mantel's house, Ian continued to gently quiz Edda about whether or not she was working for the resistance. She denied it all, laughing off his questions, even though she would have loved to impress her brother by telling him that she had delivered *De Oranjekrant* for Dr Visser 't Hooft. She longed to hear that Ian was proud of her. But she didn't say a word.

Then one day Ian arrived to collect Edda from the hospital at the end of her shift. She was worried he'd come to nose around, find out more.

"Why are you here?" she asked him.

"Eggs," Ian replied. "Mum's heard that there are some eggs at the Molenaar farm. She wants us to go together."

"OK," Edda said, slipping her arm into Ian's so that they could walk side by side out of the village towards the woods and the fields beyond, as always avoiding the main street or anywhere there might be a German soldier.

It would be good if they could get some eggs – something to supplement the official rations they were allowed from the shops. Edda felt constantly hungry. And a walk before the curfew would be fun.

"Let's try to get our hands on some eggs before that 'gang of thieves' take them all," Ian said. Another phrase the Dutch used to describe the Germans.

They walked out of the village, seeing Nazi propaganda posters pasted onto the walls of a public building. Road signs were also in German now, not

just Dutch. Ian pointed out that some of the posters had already been defaced with large white Vs.

Vs for victory.

Edda was so happy to be with Ian that she began to skip. A part of her wanted to dance alongside him now that they were out of the village and on the tracks that led through the farmland. But then he stopped her, his hand on her shoulder.

"Wait," Ian said, gesturing for her to look further up the road.

Edda frowned as she saw a couple of Germans up ahead at a checkpoint. Just the sight of their grey uniforms made her feel sick with nerves. Ian was right. They needed to be careful.

The sister and brother easily avoided the German checkpoint, walking round the edge of a field, then back onto the track. It was one of those tracks that was hard to reach from the fields

because of high and dense hedgerows and trees, but they found a way.

As they walked in silence, putting distance between themselves and the German soldiers, Edda heard a new noise. A low rumbling. And now a truck appeared ahead of them on the track.

Edda and Ian moved to step out of its way. As they did so, they heard shouting from inside the truck. In Dutch. "*Run! Arbeitseinsatz!*"

Edda froze.

Arbeitseinsatz. The German word for taking men over the age of eighteen, transporting them to Germany and forcing them to work in factories.

But she was only fourteen and Ian just seventeen. He was still a boy. Not a man. Surely they wouldn't take him?

Edda's heart stopped as she turned to see soldiers from the checkpoint coming towards them.

And now Ian was running, his footsteps scattering stones on the track as the truck approached from the other direction. Edda had no time to think. Like her brother, she acted on instinct and moved into the middle of the track to stand in the vehicle's way.

The truck stopped a metre short of Edda, more soldiers piling out, rifles in their hands. Edda turned slightly to look for Ian, hoping to see him scampering across the fields, free, too far away for the German soldiers to catch him.

But instead, Ian was standing in the road. He had run barely fifty metres. Edda didn't understand what she was seeing. Why would he stop? He could still escape, couldn't he?

She was about to call out to him when she saw the reason.

He had soldiers on one side of him, the truck on the other. And because of the dense hedgerows on

either side, her brother was trapped. He could not reach the fields to escape.

"He's only seventeen," Edda shouted as the soldiers closed in on her brother. "He's only seventeen ..."

Now – animated again – Ian began to move in short bursts from one side of the track to the other, like a trapped animal scrambling to escape. But there was no way out.

Edda heard the soldiers from the truck laughing. They didn't even raise their rifles. She was forced to watch them catch her brother, two soldiers grabbing his arms, then his legs as he dropped to the ground, twisting and turning, screaming out with rage.

Edda ran towards her brother. But there was not enough time. Ian had already been loaded onto the back of the truck and without a pause the vehicle sped away from Velp in the direction of the border with Germany.

The soldiers from the checkpoint walked back to their post and Edda was left alone, stunned, hearing the chatter of birds high above her in the woods.

And then she was running. Down the track, out of the woods, past the first houses of the village, not stopping until she found herself scrambling into the back garden, tearing her dress on some brambles or a fence post.

"Mum!"

She ran across the grass, tears streaming down her face, edging round the rose beds.

She knew that Mum and Aunt Miesje would be sitting at the back of the house, drinking tea as they always did at this time of day. And she knew they would hear her sobbing as she made her way towards them to deliver the terrible news.

"What is it?" Mum was already halfway across the lawn, breathless.

"They took him."

Mum stared back at Edda. "Took him? Took who?"

"Ian."

"Who took him?"

Edda could barely speak, half-formed noises coming from her mouth.

"Tell me. Tell me!" Edda's mum grabbed her and shook her.

"*Arbeitseinsatz*," Edda said at last.

Edda would never forget the look on her mother's face as she understood that her youngest son had been taken away by the Nazis. First there was sorrow in her eyes. Then Mum collapsed onto the lawn, threw her head back on the wet grass and covered her face with her hands.

Edda stood over her and watched, silent. Not knowing what to do next. She noticed Aunt Miesje

still sitting by the back door of the house, her head in her hands.

It was impossible. For all of them. Impossible and unbearable.

Mum sat up and put her hand out to Edda. "Help me up."

Edda helped her. Still paralysed inside. She couldn't think or say anything.

They hugged. A tight hug that hurt to give and to receive. Edda could feel her mum's bony arms digging into her.

*

Later that evening, after Mum, Aunt Miesje and Opa had sat staring at the floor for what seemed like hours, Mum broke the silence.

"Tell Dr Visser 't Hooft that we'll do the dark evening," she whispered.

SEVEN

It was late as Edda and her mum stepped out into the dark lanes of Velp. The sun was long gone. The curfew had been in place for over an hour.

Edda had never felt so determined. Since seeing Ian captured by the Nazis for *Arbeitseinsatz*, all she had thought about was this night. Every doubt about working for the resistance had gone.

The chatter of anti-aircraft fire masked the noise of their footsteps as they walked towards the house where Edda would dance. High above them in the night sky, British aircraft flew over the Netherlands, on their way to bomb Germany, searchlights criss-crossing each other as the Germans tried to locate them.

Edda was struck by the thought that this creeping around at night no longer felt unusual. It had become normal to skulk about in the dark, living beneath the flightpaths of Allied bombers.

Under her overcoat, Edda was wearing a costume that her mother had spent most of the last week sewing for her performance tonight. Not used to the cumbersome fabric and the way it draped around her legs and arms, Edda stumbled, kicking a stone against something metal. There was a loud clang and Edda's heart jumped.

Her mum shushed her. "We have to be quiet and careful."

"I know." Edda rolled her eyes. If only her mum knew that she had delivered newsletters for Dr Visser 't Hooft several times now, perhaps

she would stop treating Edda like a child.

But Edda said nothing. She couldn't. Her mum had enough to worry about. She'd been so sad recently. And how could she be anything but sad? Her youngest son was a slave in Germany. Mum had no idea if he was safe, if he was being fed, if an Allied bomb had fallen on him and killed him. And she rarely saw Alex, her other son – only on the few occasions he was able to visit them secretly at night from wherever he was hiding at the time.

Edda missed both her brothers intensely. *That's why I have to do this*, she said to herself. *I will not be nervous. I will not be sad. I will put on a smile and dance. And the better I dance, the more money we will raise for the resistance, and the sooner we can drive the Germans out of the Netherlands.*

She looked up at the skies again and thought of the hundreds of bombers on their way to help

defeat Germany. They were doing their bit. Now she would do hers.

Mother and daughter approached a large blacked-out house that Edda had walked past a hundred times. As they got closer, she could see other people making their way through the unlit streets, walking in pairs or alone, looking forward to a night of entertainment and community.

Edda was surprised and delighted to see a girl from her dance class arriving at the same time – Anje. Anje was one of the few local children Edda could call a friend. When she had arrived from England, Edda had struggled to speak Dutch, and people laughed at her for the way she said some words. Not Anje. Anje was kind, and she had the sweetest little black-and-white dog, Roos, that Edda loved to play with.

Edda had not expected to see Anje here tonight,

and both girls grinned broadly, waiting till they
were inside before greeting each other.

Silently they were ushered in, and the door
closed behind them.

Close to a hundred people were gathered in
a large, dimly lit room, some sitting on chairs and
sofas, some squatting on the floor and others still
standing.

All were silent.

Edda's heart leaped in her chest when she saw
Alex. Her brother was there! Broad shouldered, his
blond hair combed back from his face. Edda noticed
that he was wearing farming clothes and wondered
if that was what he was doing now. Helping a farmer
in return for a safe place to stay, perhaps? Or were
the farming clothes a disguise? Wasn't it more likely
that he was working for the resistance and the
clothes helped him blend in as an essential farming

worker? It made her wonder who else here had jobs for the resistance like she did. They might all do. She would never know.

Seeing her gaze across at him, Alex waved excitedly, and Edda wanted to call out but knew she couldn't make a sound. She waved back and wished she could run over for a big hug. Later, she hoped.

*

After some music and a softly read poem, Edda stood, ready to perform her dance. She had choreographed it herself, aware she would not have a large space to move around in. A heavy blanket covered the piano to mute its noise, and the windows were fully blacked out.

There was no sign to the outside world that this gathering was happening. Those taking part – including Edda and her mum – were breaking two

important rules laid down by their occupiers.

First, they were failing to observe the curfew and were out of their houses later than was permitted. Second, they were supporting the resistance. If they were discovered, the organisers would be punished. Maybe executed. They would certainly be tortured. And first on the list for that treatment would be Dr Visser 't Hooft, whom Edda had spotted talking to members of the audience earlier.

Edda pushed her worries to the back of her mind as the piano music began. Chopin. Soft and gentle; slow and quiet.

As soon as the first notes played, she felt it. That sense of wonder she experienced when she was dancing. All her excitement and fear and anger evaporated. Edda was completely in the moment, moving to the music, to her choreography, careful

to land as silently as possible, conscious she was breathless and felt a little shaky.

I'm hungry, she thought as she danced. *I'm always hungry.*

As Edda tried to focus on her sequence of moves, she found that she could not ignore the faces of the audience and how they were responding to the music and her movement. She noticed little flashes of orange among the crowd. Handkerchiefs in top pockets. Scarves around necks. Orange was the colour of the Dutch royal family – forced into exile by the Nazis. And now it was the colour of resistance. It was the absolute opposite of grey – the colour of occupation and tyranny.

When the piece came to its slow and delicate end, Edda was met with silence. No applause. No calls for more. There could be no unnecessary noise. But she could see that many eyes were

glistening in the dim light. She smiled, then curtsied.

After a couple of seconds, the silence was broken by the sound of sobbing from a man in the front row. He had his face buried in his coat. A chair creaked as someone leaned over to comfort him. Edda wondered who he was and what had happened for him to react to her dance with such emotion.

*

Later, after the performers had finished, Edda watched Dr Visser 't Hooft pass a hat around for donations and caught the looks on the faces of couples as they silently agreed what they could afford to give. It was obvious how much people looked up to the doctor. They respected him, admired him. Edda understood why he was passing the hat round himself and not getting someone else to do it. These people would do anything for

Dr Visser 't Hooft, would dig deeper into their pockets to give him money. Would even risk their lives for him. She knew that.

Edda noticed her mother discreetly put some notes in the hat and felt a sudden rush of joy. Here was her mum publicly supporting the resistance. Giving money. Letting her daughter dance. It was clear what side her mum was on, wasn't it? It was obvious she was a woman who could be trusted.

Soon the hat was full. Edda felt exhausted as Alex came over and hugged her, said he was proud, that she was the best sister in the world and that he missed her every day. Edda couldn't remember feeling so happy. Not for a long time. Alex kissed the top of her head and then he was gone, leaving Edda to wonder when she would see him again.

And then it was time to go home. Edda felt increasingly tired as she walked in silence next to

Mum, who was bubbling over with pride at seeing Edda dance.

They would have to be quick and quiet. The curfew had been in place for hours now. If they were caught, they'd be in huge trouble.

EIGHT

Edda and her mum walked home arm in arm, talking first about Alex. They used the quietest voices so as not to attract the attention of any stray German patrols, though it was so dark it was unlikely they would be seen. They agreed that he had looked well, seemed happy. Neither speculated about what he might be doing dressed in farming clothes. They just enthused about how they would all be together again one day. Mum and Alex and Ian and Edda.

Edda was acutely aware that her mum was clinging to her tightly and thought about how she

was now the only one of Mum's children that she could walk with, talk with.

Then Mum spoke again, sounding serious.

"Edda?"

"Yes?"

Both were whispering so as not to be heard.

"I was proud of you tonight."

"It was nice to dance again," Edda said.

"I don't just mean the dancing."

"Oh?"

Edda waited for her mum to speak. She knew something important was coming. Mum was struggling to find the words. And that meant she was feeling emotional and didn't quite know how to express herself. Her mother was like that. A great talker until it came to the things that really mattered.

"You were brave," Mum told her. "What you did tonight was brave. If we'd been found, we'd have

been in trouble. But you have done something good – I mean ... raising money to help those poor people. I was proud of you."

They had stopped walking and were standing away from the road, near the stream that ran in a channel from the woods and through the gardens, towards the great river south of Velp. The Rhine.

Edda turned to face her mum. She felt proud of her mum too. For letting her support the resistance. And deep down she felt a huge sense of relief that Mum was on the right side. But there was one question still unresolved.

"Mum. There's something that's been worrying me, and I need to ask you about it."

Mum hesitated. "Then ask," she said.

Edda swallowed. "There was a photograph of you that I remember. Taken on the day you met Hitler."

Mum paused for several seconds.

"Yes. I did meet Hitler." Mum spoke in the quietest of voices. "We had a photograph taken afterwards. That's the one you remember. It was a long time ago."

"But why?" Edda managed to say. "Why did you meet him?"

"I will tell you, my love. And I will be honest." There was a tension in Mum's voice. As if she was struggling to get the words out.

"Before the war, I was attracted to what Hitler said. I believed that he was going to make Germany great again. And Europe. But what I have seen since then – in our village and in Arnhem and what happened to your uncle and now to your brothers – these things have made me realise I was a fool."

Edda felt a rush of relief. Her mum was not a sympathiser; she didn't belong on the list in the resistance newsletter.

"What happened to the photograph?" Edda asked.

"I threw it away," Mum said.

Edda didn't speak.

"There's something else," Mum went on. "You need to be careful. There are lots of people who want to help the resistance. We saw many of them tonight. And I am one. But some people do still support the Germans. There are thousands of women and men in this country who are members of the Dutch Nazi Party. Even some on our street. So be careful who sees you when you're running errands for Dr Visser 't Hooft, if that's what you're doing. The Allies will be coming soon. We just need to be careful as the Germans will be all the more desperate to stop the resistance."

As they set off again to walk the short distance home, Edda's mind was running riot with questions.

Did Mum know Edda did other things to help Dr Visser 't Hooft? Her words implied that she did. Edda wanted to tell her mum everything. She was desperate to. But she wouldn't. She had promised.

They walked the rest of the way in silence. For the first time in ages, Edda felt good. Like her mum approved of her. Like she approved of her mum. Like they had done something to help.

Now she had a taste to do more. She would be brave again and again if she could feel like this.

NINE

It was a hot June day in 1944, and Edda was in the steamy hospital auxiliary room, trying to ignore the growling of her stomach and the weakness she felt in her arms and legs. She was hungry. Always hungry.

There was so little food now that ration cards gave people only half the calories they needed. Most people made up the rest by growing their own vegetables and by making flour from peas or even from tulip bulbs dug up from the garden. Edda had started to give dance lessons to younger children

and sometimes their families would give her food in return.

This was how they lived.

Using what energy she had to wash the bandages, Edda worked on. But she was distracted by shouts and the sound of laughter. She saw two of the nurses hugging in the corridor. What was going on?

Suddenly Dr Visser 't Hooft entered the laundry room, his eyes glistening.

"Have you heard?" he asked, grinning.

"No," Edda replied. "Nothing. What is it?"

"The Allies have landed in Normandy," Dr Visser 't Hooft told her. He was breathless with excitement. "Remember this day, Edda: 6 June 1944. There are Allied boots on the ground in northern Europe."

"What?"

"In France, right now, there are tens of thousands of men landing on the beaches, invading

France. The British. Americans. Canadians. They are all here now. They have a foothold in Europe and the Germans are on the run!"

"How far away are they?" Edda had dropped her tongs and was staring at the doctor.

"A few hundred kilometres. It's just a matter of time, Edda, before we are liberated. This is a great day."

*

Edda ran home after she had finished her work at the hospital. She was no longer able to use her bicycle for fear that the Germans would snatch it from her as she rode it. As she ran, she imagined Allied soldiers emerging from the sea and dropping from the sky using parachutes. Lines and lines of them dressed in khaki uniforms, as soldiers in grey ran back to Germany, ending the war.

She saw more people out walking than usual,

some with orange handkerchiefs in pockets on their chests, subtly placed so they could hide them if the Germans appeared. The villagers were animated, excited.

Back at home she found Mum and Opa talking to some of the neighbours in the garden, holding mugs of coffee. Real coffee. Edda had not smelled real coffee for months.

"Where's that from?" she gasped.

"I kept it for a special occasion," Opa told her. "We have friends with feet on the ground, Edda. What could be more special?"

Mum's eyes were red. "Ian will be able to come home soon," she stuttered. "And Alex out of hiding. Soon we'll be able to sit around a table together and all of us will drink coffee. Good coffee."

*

As the summer passed, Allied soldiers moved inland, creating a new feeling among the people of Velp.

Hope.

It was something they had not felt for a long time. But Edda identified signs in the skies and on the streets every day which made her feel that soon the war would be over.

American bombers flew high overhead during the daytime, heading east to attack German factories. These great swarms of aircraft gave Edda a thrill.

And every night the radio at Jan Mantel's brought news of Allied advances. They had taken Paris, most of France, then moved north into Belgium and across the Dutch border, closer and closer to Velp. So close you could hear explosions from the front line.

Soon life would be normal again. Edda couldn't wait to be free of the Germans. To have her brothers

home. To be able to eat properly and dance. To have her life back.

On the downside, after the Allied invasion, Velp had become the new German base in the east of the Netherlands. Enemy soldiers were everywhere, forced back from France and Belgium and the south. These soldiers were bedraggled. Hungry. Stealing the harvest from the fields. Looting shops. Nazi officers took houses from Dutch families, turfing them out onto the street.

Sometimes British fighter planes swooped down and had a go at some of the Germans, forcing the enemy to park their tanks under trees outside family homes. To hide. To cower.

This pleased Edda. She liked to see the Germans being attacked. Even if it felt dangerous to be in the firing line.

At night, as she listened out for the British

bombers heading for Germany, she smiled,
fantasising about what good news would come next,
sometimes remembering Ian's prediction that, in
time, paratroopers would arrive to liberate them.

And then, one day, it happened.

TEN

They were outside the house, eating lunch, when Edda heard different sounds to the noises of war they had become used to.

It was a slow Sunday in September. Summer was over, but Opa liked to eat outside on a Sunday until the weather was too cold to bear. Edda loved eating outside too. She smiled at her grandfather, mum and aunt as they ate bread her aunt had made from pea flour, as well as soup cooked from nettles that Edda had gathered from the back lanes. Some of the roses were still in bloom, but most of the vegetables had already been harvested, leaving large patches of dark earth cut into what was once an expansive lawn.

The unusual sounds of war became louder.

"What is that?" Edda asked, her head on one side, frowning. There was a droning noise and sporadic cracks of gunfire far in the distance. But all louder than usual.

"The Americans flying to Germany?" Mum suggested.

"No. It's different," Edda said, and stood up to walk across the lawn so that she could see to the east, round the side of the house.

Edda stopped and put hands to her mouth when she saw that the planes she had been hearing were lower than usual. Much lower. Barely higher than the treetops, dangerously within range of the German defences. There were puffs of smoke in the air. And something else, something

new. Hundreds of tiny dots against the bright afternoon sky.

"There are dots," Edda said, knowing she wasn't making sense.

"What do you mean, dots?" Mum asked.

Opa was on his feet.

Edda could hear noises of cheering now too. And she understood. It was happening.

"They're here," she shouted.

"Who's here?"

"The paratroopers Ian said would come."

And now, grinning wildly, she grabbed her mum's hand and pulled her across the lawn to see that there were hundreds – no, thousands – of dots, of men falling out of aeroplanes and to the ground.

Opa was with them now. "They're dropping into Arnhem," he gasped. "This side of the Rhine. Come on."

Without closing up the house, Edda and her family ran onto their front lawn to be met by smiling faces on the main road, cheering, the fluttering of orange. Always orange.

This was it. The day they had dreamed of. The day that meant the war would be over. That freedom was in sight. Soon they could be happy again.

Edda felt like she would explode with joy when she saw Alex running up the lane to them, still dressed in farmer's clothes. Edda ran to him and leaped into his arms, then Alex swung her round and round. How long had it been since she'd seen him?

"You're safe," Edda said into his neck. "You're safe."

She was laughing and crying and chattering at the same time.

Then there was a sudden loud noise, a revving and a rumbling. Everyone stood aside as three

trucks loaded with German troops sped through the village, towards Arnhem, to take on the liberators. Alex dodged behind a wall.

"Pesky *moffen*," he muttered.

Edda laughed and laughed. She couldn't stop herself. Then she danced around the street with the other children for a while, but stopped when she saw her opa and Alex talking seriously to two other older men, one of them Jan Mantel. Mum was with them too.

Edda quickly broke away from the celebrations. She could tell her family were planning something, even though she could not hear their words.

"What is it?" she asked.

Mum replied, "Your grandfather and Alex are going into Arnhem, across the fields. With Jan and Cees. Just to find out what's happening in town. From a distance."

"I'll go too," Edda said, beaming.

Her grandfather put a hand on her shoulder. "No, it's a dangerous mission."

"Is Alex going?"

"Yes."

"Then I will too."

"No," Mum said.

"Please."

"No," Mum said again.

Edda stepped back, stunned into silence. She frowned as she watched the men tying the strings that had replaced the laces on their boots. Both Opa and Alex looked thin, Edda noticed. Jan Mantel too. She looked at her own arms. Thinner too, like everyone else. War was diminishing them all week by week, month by month.

Edda sat on the front step and watched the men prepare to leave. How annoying was this?

But once they had gone, and Edda was left with Mum and Aunt Miesje, her frustration turned into fear as she heard the rattles and cracks of warfare echoing towards her village.

Alex and Opa were walking into a warzone. Anything could happen. What if she never saw them again?

ELEVEN

The next few hours were spent sitting around the stove in the kitchen and listening. To the thud of explosions, the scream of shells, the drone of aeroplanes. The telephone lines had been cut off by the Germans, along with the electricity, gas and water. There was nothing to do but wait and worry. They couldn't even go to Jan Mantel's to listen to *Radio Oranje* and catch up with any news.

Edda had no idea what was happening. To her town. To her family. To her future. Her mind was full of dark fears about the fate of two of the people

she loved most in the world. Why had they let Alex and Opa go?

Now it was dark they could see quite clearly that the horizon to the south-west was lit up in a blazing orange, but this was not the light of the setting sun. Arnhem was burning. Edda worried also about friends she had in the city. Like Anje, her former dance partner.

German trucks carrying soldiers thundered through the village all night. Sometimes away from the battle, sometimes towards it. With no news and such confusing signs, no one knew whether the Netherlands had been liberated or not.

That night they slept in the cellar for the first time. Or tried to. Deep under the big house was a series of barrel-vaulted cellars for keeping things cool, including wine and meats. Cellars that had been empty of food and drink for months now. The ceilings

were made of bricks packed in with mortar. Stone slabs on the floor. It was better than an air-raid shelter, and they felt as safe as anywhere in Velp.

Mum, Aunt Miesje and Edda had dragged mattresses down from the bedrooms, as well as chairs and some blankets, Mum's sewing basket and a table. They lit candles, giving them enough light to see each other by and for Mum to repair some of Edda's clothes. Close up to the light, Edda could see her sketchbook, where she drew dancers. Now that the lessons she had enjoyed during the early years of the war had stopped, this was one of the few things she could still do to immerse herself in dance.

But the accompaniment of the sounds of war made it impossible to forget what was happening in the nearby city and in the skies above.

Edda had worked out by now what each of the sounds was.

A rumbling growing louder then fading was a German troop truck.

The crackle of rapid gunfire meant that Allied aircraft were flying overhead and the Germans were firing at them with their anti-aircraft guns.

A scream or whistling sound was a shell being fired from one side to the other.

Somehow it felt better to be able to identify the noises, but Edda couldn't help thinking how odd it was that they were just sitting there, sketching and sewing, as tanks and trucks smashed up the roads outside, bullets and shells flew all over the place and no doubt some aeroplanes were burning as they fell out of the sky.

And yet it was the silences that were harder to bear. Silence meant that a noise was about to come. But what noise? And what would that noise mean and bring down on them?

Then there was a loud crash. Quite close. After jumping with shock, Edda looked straight into her mum's eyes.

"Damn *moffen*!" Mum swore. "The sooner they are gone the better for all of us." Then she went back to her sewing.

Edda stared at her sketchbook and tried not to let her thoughts overcome her. Her worries. What would Velp look like in the morning? Would there be anything left? Anyone? Were Opa and Alex alive? Would she even be alive to see the next day?

*

Opa returned at dawn, his clothes dusty and dirty. The air was cool, and mist hung in wisps around the tops of the trees. A heavy dew had settled on the grass overnight.

"What happened? What did you see? Are you

OK? Are we free?" Edda fired questions at Opa like bullets, but suddenly realised her brother wasn't there. "And where's Alex?" she added urgently.

"Come in and sit down, Edda," Opa said. "I'll tell you all together." His voice sounded weary, Edda noticed. Something wasn't right.

Edda, Mum and Aunt Miesje followed Opa from the doorstep into the sitting room. They sat in a circle round the coffee table. Mum brought a bottle of beer and opened it, then poured Opa a glass. Opa watched silently before taking a long drink. Then he spoke.

"There is a fierce battle taking place," Opa said. "And parts of Arnhem are smashed to pieces."

"Where's Alex?" Edda asked again.

"Safe. I'm sorry, Edda. He's back in hiding."

Edda took a deep breath and didn't say anything. She had so wanted to see Alex again. But it

was enough to know that he was safe. She had to be satisfied with that.

Then Mum asked a question. "What more can you tell us?"

Opa coughed and shook his head. "The British are here. Hundreds of them. Maybe thousands. But the Germans are not defeated. Not at all."

Another pause. Another long drink of beer. Edda felt all that hope that the occupation might be over drain away.

Mum refilled Opa's glass.

"There is a ground war, and it could quite easily come this way." Opa's voice was deadly serious.

"What must we do?" Mum asked him.

"We stay here. We prepare for war passing through our village – when we will either have to run or hide. Pack some bags in case we need to go. But for now we stay put."

War in Velp?

Edda wondered what that meant. Gunfire and shells on their lane? In their garden? Could that really happen?

TWELVE

As Opa had suggested, the whole family stayed in the cellar for three days and nights, listening to the sound of war raging just a couple of kilometres down the road in Arnhem.

How were the Allies getting on after they had parachuted in? It was impossible to tell. German aircraft came low over Velp every hour, followed a few seconds later by the sound of explosions in Arnhem.

Would the war spread east to Velp? It was hard to predict. If it did, their bags were packed and they were ready to flee. Or to try to.

When Edda woke on the fourth morning, it was

dark in the unlit cellar, apart from a shaft of light coming down the steps. She lay quietly for some time, listening. But there was nothing to be heard. Only the sounds of her family sleeping broke the silence. No explosions. No gunfire. Nothing.

Perhaps, she thought, the battle was over. Perhaps they had been liberated overnight.

"I need a drink," Mum said, seeing Edda awake.

"Let me get you one," Edda suggested. "I'll be up and down in no time. It's very quiet now."

Mum nodded. "Thank you, my love. But be careful. If you hear anything, get back down here. Forget water. Forget everything. Understood?"

"Yes, Mum."

Edda crept up the wooden staircase from the cellar and towards the light coming through the windows at the back of the house, happy to be doing something.

Before getting water, she decided to check what was left of their village. Edda had no idea what to expect as she opened the back door. Would the world have been destroyed? Would there be nothing but rubble and charred masonry? Or would there be signs of hope? Allied soldiers patrolling the streets maybe?

Stepping outside, Edda was met with silence, apart from birdsong and the cough-like call of a male deer in the woods to the north of the village. For the first time in days, there were no sounds of battle, but she could smell war. The stench of burning filled her nostrils and mouth.

She retched. Urgh. It was horrible. One of the things she loved best about living where they did, out in the countryside, was the smell of nature, flowers and fields and fresh air. There was none of that today.

And then she heard a new sound. Instinctively,

Edda crept to the corner of the house and looked down the road towards the village centre in the direction of what she had decided sounded like marching feet.

Was this the moment? The moment she saw thousands of German soldiers marching home defeated, retreating? The day she could begin to believe she'd see Ian and Alex again, safe, at home?

Excited at the thought and forgetting the danger, Edda scampered across the lawn and watched a column of men in dirty-green uniforms approach. All of them unarmed. They were guarded by a grey German soldier every twenty metres, a gun at his side, forcing them on.

The faces of the men were smudged dark with mud or ash. They were prisoners, Edda realised. Bewildered British paratroopers.

The liberation of Arnhem had failed.

Full of disappointment and pity for the defeated soldiers she was watching, Edda wanted to say something. To call across to the men. But what? What do you say to men who have been through hell and are now prisoners of war?

Thank you for trying, maybe?

Edda didn't have any words. She said nothing.

As she stood there, stunned, some of the men saw her and smiled. Others winked but made no obvious gestures. Then two of the men walking side by side gave the V for victory sign and, remembering Ian and his V signs, Edda couldn't help but let out a laugh. The kind of laugh where you nearly cry as well.

Even though her hopes of being liberated had been dashed, she found herself doing her best to smile at these defeated soldiers as they trudged along the dry lane.

Towards the back of the column of men was

a tall soldier who wore a red beret at a jaunty angle. Seeing her peering over the wall at him, the paratrooper called out, "Don't worry, miss. We're coming back – that's a promise."

*

It wasn't many days later when Edda heard the sound of footsteps on the road again. At first she hoped that the British soldier was keeping his promise. But she knew that couldn't be true. The invasion of Arnhem had failed, and the Germans were more in control than ever. All the paratroopers she'd seen would be in prison camps in Germany, maybe even being forced to work like Ian.

And the noise on the front road this time was not the orderly footsteps of British soldiers marching anyway. It was a slow, scratching, stumbling noise.

Edda went down the drive to see what was

happening. She was faced with what looked like a river of people, of rumbling trolleys, prams and bicycles with flat tyres.

These were not soldiers; they were ordinary people. Civilians. It seemed like the whole population of Arnhem was descending on Velp. The most miserable sight Edda had seen in her life.

THIRTEEN

Miserable was the right word, Edda thought, watching the stream of people straggling their way through Velp as a light rain fell on the village.

Mum was standing next to her now, watching women, children, old men. Some were wearing multiple layers, as if they had tried to put on all their clothes at once. Others carried white flags pinned to their jackets as they lugged bags or pulled handcarts behind them. A few had dogs. Others, sheep and goats. Babies were crying. Adults were crying. Young and old, each of them looked filthy and shattered.

"The Germans are emptying Arnhem," Mum told Edda. "We must do what we can to help these poor souls."

It was a desperate sight for Edda to take in. But it was not the chaotic look of these people that upset her the most – it was that expression on their faces. Their wide eyes stared at the world around them in confusion.

"But why?" Edda asked. "Why can't they stay in Arnhem? The battle is over."

"I can only imagine it's so that the Germans can root out any Allied paratroopers," Mum replied, glancing at one man among the refugees who was wearing a scarf over his head and limping heavily as if he had suffered an injury. "Like him," Mum whispered. "I suspect."

"What will we do with him?" Edda asked.

"The same as with the others we can help,"

Mum said. "Give him a blanket, some food. He's welcome here. We'll shelter as many as we can."

Mum walked towards the mass of people and ushered some of them towards the house. Edda watched, feeling helpless as thirty or more refugees came into their garden. One group looked particularly shabby, pulling a pram loaded with their possessions behind them, a dog trotting along beside a woman and three children. They looked pathetic and dirty, Edda thought. She felt herself recoil, although she tried not to show it.

Then she saw that the dog – a small black-and-white thing – was wagging its tail at her. As if it knew her.

Roos. It was Roos. Anje's dog. From Arnhem. And for a few moments, Edda could not work out why Roos was with this group of bedraggled refugees. Until she looked properly at the person holding the dog's lead.

Anje! It was Anje. Her friend. With her sisters and mother. Edda gasped, then ran to Anje, ashamed she had not recognised her immediately.

*

That night the population of Velp increased thirty times over. The people of the village took in as many refugees as they could. Houses were full. Churches were full. The public buildings that the Germans had not taken over were full. Locals shared any food and medical supplies they had with the refugees.

There were nearly forty people staying at Edda's, including Anje and her sisters and mother. Some lodged in the house. Others in the cellar. Many sheltered in the garden under tarpaulins Opa had found in his shed. The garden now looked like a camping ground, with small fires burning as people cooked food that local farmers brought into the village for them.

Anje seemed broken. She told Edda that when she saw the paratroopers dropping in and when the British initially took control and drove the Germans out, she had expected liberation, freedom, a world back to normal where she could enjoy her life again. Now she had lost everything – her toys, her clothes, her home.

"We hid in the cellar and a shell came down on the house. We thought we would be buried alive. The ceiling collapsed. Look at me. I'm covered in dust. Then, earlier today, we were made to leave. The Germans forced us out. At gunpoint."

Edda stroked her friend's hair, picking pieces of dust and plaster out of it.

"I saw bodies," Anje confessed after a long pause.

"Bodies?" Edda asked.

"Dead bodies. There was one in the street outside my house," Anje said. "It was pale and stiff and it was covered in dust and dirt and I couldn't help thinking, *That could be me.* That I could be left lying like that in a street one day. That we all could."

Later that evening, Dr Visser 't Hooft called round on his motorbike to ask if Edda would come to help at the hospital. But after seeing the dozens of refugees Edda's family were caring for, the doctor changed his mind. He sniffed the air, smelling the cooking food.

"You're feeding them all?" he asked, astonished.

Edda nodded. "Local farmers have brought food. We made beet pancakes and nettle soup. A five-star menu," she tried to joke.

Dr Visser 't Hooft laughed. "I see now why you have been detained. You must stay here. Help your mother."

Edda saw him glance at the man with the scarf wrapped around his head, sitting alone, making tea

on a fire at the far end of the garden. The man who had been limping.

"You need to hide him inside, Edda," Dr Visser 't Hooft whispered. "He's a paratrooper. British. The Germans will make hell if they find you harbouring him. Has your mother realised? Should I take him with me?"

Edda shook her head. "Leave him here. We're going to hide him."

"You know what the Germans will do if they find him?" Dr Visser 't Hooft asked. "To you? To your mother?"

Edda swallowed. "Mum said we're to look after him."

"God bless her," he said. "I'm glad to know you and your mother. Thank you."

The doctor straddled his motorbike, then hesitated, glancing around him to make sure no one

was listening. Edda studied him. He looked tired and thin. Like everyone else, Edda thought. War was like a disease and they were all wasting away. Maybe, she thought, Anje was right and they would all end up lying in the street covered in a layer of dust one day.

"From time to time ..." the doctor began in a quiet voice.

Edda waited for him to continue.

"... one of our American or British friends lands in the woods nearby. We need to reach them. But it helps very much if whoever goes to them speaks English."

"I speak English," Edda said.

"I know." Dr Visser 't Hooft smiled. "I'd like you to think whether that is something you would be willing to do. The enemy ... they would not expect a child to be able to do something so brave. But I know

you are very brave and can help, maybe. Though ... please ... don't answer me now. Think about it."

Edda nodded, then watched Dr Visser 't Hooft speed away on his motorbike.

How things had changed. Edda remembered the resistance newsletter that had listed her mother as a person not to be trusted. And how that had made her feel. But now she knew that Dr Visser 't Hooft trusted her and her mother. He had said he was glad to know them.

Edda smiled to herself as she turned to go back to helping the refugees from Arnhem. For weeks she had felt that she could do nothing but watch the war happen around her; now she felt like she could do something good by helping the refugees and maybe she could go even further to help the doctor with stranded airmen.

If he ever needed her, she would be ready.

FOURTEEN

Among the refugees staying in the various rooms and the garden of Opa's house, there were fourteen children. Most aged between five and twelve. From the squabbles breaking out among them as they waited, not knowing what would happen to them next, it was clear to Edda and her mum that they were bored and needed to be entertained.

"I have an idea," Mum said, studying the children for a while. "What if you use one of the rooms upstairs to teach some of the children to dance?"

Edda grinned. How wonderful would that be? She had loved teaching the village children to dance,

and this would be like having her very own dance school – sort of. She agreed immediately.

Opa built a barre along the longer wall of his bedroom and made sure the rest of his furniture was cleared out to create an area for dancing and a narrow space behind a false wall where the British paratrooper could be hidden.

"There." Mum smiled. "And it will give our secret guest something to listen to until we can find a way to get him safely out of here."

The lessons began the next morning, light streaming in through the open windows. Edda had the children clapping in time to the music and working on stretching exercises to make their muscles more supple for dancing. She taught them how to play a role, using their faces and bodies to pretend they were something they were not. But most of all she tried to make this part of the day feel

like fun, allowing them to forget their troubles for a while.

Anje helped by winding the gramophone player to keep the music going. At one point Edda thought she heard the hidden paratrooper tapping his feet to keep time. She would have to warn him not to do that.

Edda was teaching her third class of the day when they arrived. A large truck thundering up the road, skidding to a halt, German soldiers jumping out, shouting. They were always shouting.

"Wo ist der Engländer?" Where is the Englishman?

Edda felt an overwhelming surge of panic. The enemy had come looking for British paratroopers. What if they found him? What would they do? She knew all too well. The punishment for hiding a British soldier would be brutal.

Anje had frozen on hearing the Germans arrive, no longer operating the gramophone player, afraid of what would come next.

"Keep winding." Edda whispered encouragement to her friend, coming back to the moment, knowing that she had to stand up to the Germans now or everything would be lost. "And keep dancing. All of you," she said to the children.

The music resumed, and the children began to dance tentatively as the sound of boots on the floor and stairs grew louder.

"*Wo ist der Engländer?*" came the shout again.

And then they were in the doorway. Three Nazis. Edda could smell their sour soldier sweat. All had machine guns pointed at the children.

Edda was terrified the Germans would find the pilot. Scared too for the children. She turned to them.

"Sit on the floor, all of you," she instructed.

The children sat, many now crying in fear.

Edda stood in front of her tiny cowering dancers while attempting to look outraged, facing the soldiers and their guns as if she were a character in a dance. Trying to do the thing she had encouraged the children to do: to play a role. A heroine challenging a villain. To pretend she was brave and strong. She hoped that the children would look small on the floor, small and vulnerable, so the soldiers might feel ashamed and leave.

The seconds ticked by. None of the three soldiers spoke. Nor did they step into the room.

And then – after glancing at each other furtively – they lowered their guns. One even attempted to smile at the children.

"*Entschuldigung*," one of the soldiers said. Excuse us.

And then they were gone.

Edda sat down on the floor among the children. Her legs felt like jelly now the danger had passed. How had she found the courage to stand up to the enemy like that?

She stared at her feet, stupefied, until she realised that one of the little dancers she'd been teaching had stood up, come over and was stroking her hair. She had to work hard not to burst into tears in front of the other children.

Edda was not sure how much more of this danger, this tension, she could face. But she knew more would come.

And she was right.

*

A day after the soldiers had been searching for the British paratrooper, the Germans declared that all

the refugees from Arnhem must move on. Every one of them. They knew there were British soldiers among the thousands of displaced people from the city, and they were determined to flush them out.

And so the children Edda had been teaching to dance had to leave. Anje too. With her family. And Roos. The paratrooper had been whisked away by Dr Visser 't Hooft the night before.

Edda embraced Anje before she left. "I'll see you when this is all over," she said.

"I hope so," Anje replied.

"We'll dance together. On a stage. One day."

Anje smiled. "I hope so," she repeated, and Edda felt a pain deep in the pit of her stomach. What would happen to each of them before they met again? Would they meet again at all?

"Please say thank you to your mum," Anje said. "For looking after us."

Edda watched Anje join her family. Mum had given them more food and water, enough to last perhaps three days.

"Where will they go?" Edda asked when the refugees had gone.

"I don't know," Mum replied. "The next village perhaps. There will be people like us who will look after them. Dutch people are good people."

Mum's words were no comfort for Edda. She feared for her friend and wondered if they would ever get the chance to dance together again. She also thought of what Anje had said about seeing the dead body covered in dust, wondering again if one day they would all end up like that.

FIFTEEN

The war rumbled on. All the hope that people had felt after the Allied invasion was gone, and now they were facing a long and difficult winter.

Everyone was hungry. Velp had shared what little food they had left with the refugees. Their rations now provided only a third of the calories they needed to survive. Could it get any worse? How would it end?

Edda and her family moved into their cellar if there was any sound of aeroplanes overhead or of air-raid sirens. They had to put up with their water and gas and electricity sometimes being cut off.

They chopped down trees for wood. Then tore down and burned fences, stripped abandoned houses of floorboards. All to burn to keep warm, but still the cold seeped into every room.

Edda was cold and hungry and, to make matters worse, she had ever more time to think about these things. Dance lessons were a distant memory and there was no school either. She worked hard at the hospital and queued outside the shops with her ration cards for the family. And she still used the barre put up in her grandfather's bedroom to continue with her own practice, but with so little food she often felt so tired she didn't have the energy to dance.

"Maybe you should give it up for the time being?" Mum suggested, glancing at Edda's legs and arms.

Edda knew she was thin now. Stick thin. She

could see her own bones. Name them like she could by looking in a textbook at school. She knew it wasn't good. But everyone looked like that.

Still, Edda would shake her head when her mother suggested quitting.

"I need it," she said.

"But you will use up all your energy. We have no food. You need to stop."

"I need to dance," Edda said again.

It was during one of these conversations early in the new year that they heard a boom above the house. Opening the back door they saw a large aeroplane screaming out of the sky, its fuselage burning, its engine roaring as it hit the woods north of Velp and then exploded. One solitary parachute could be seen descending, a silhouette against the darkening sky.

"I hope he finds somewhere safe," Opa said, his

face pale. "The Nazis will see him like we see him. And they'll be after him."

Within minutes, they heard the sound of German vehicles roaring around the lanes of Velp.

*

The morning after the plane came down, Dr Visser 't Hooft arrived on his motorbike. Mum and Edda watched as the doctor took off his helmet and approached them on the front step.

"May I speak to Edda alone?" he asked.

Edda saw alarm on her mother's face, but after glancing at her daughter, Mum nodded and stepped back.

"Of course, Doctor. Hospital business is between the two of you."

Edda walked to the far end of the lawn with Dr Visser 't Hooft until they were out of earshot.

"I have something I would like to ask you to do," Dr Visser 't Hooft said gently.

Edda knew what it was.

"Before you agree, listen," he cautioned. "I know what you said to me, but this is dangerous. I have not asked you to do something like this before. If it goes wrong, you and your mother and aunt and grandfather will suffer. All of you."

Edda knew that the doctor's warning was real. But she also knew it was likely that there was an airman nearby who needed an English speaker to help him escape to safety – an airman who had risked his life trying to defeat the Nazis.

He had been brave – now she had to be brave too.

"I'll do it," she confirmed.

SIXTEEN

Less than an hour after being given her mission by Dr Visser 't Hooft, Edda walked out of the back of her grandfather's garden, onto the lane and north towards the woods, wearing a child's coat she had been given four years before. She had been surprised to find that it still fitted her and that she was even able to hide clothes for the pilot under it. She had chosen it as she hoped that it made her look younger, less likely to be doing anything for the resistance.

Edda was well aware that what Dr Visser 't Hooft had asked her to do was extremely

dangerous. That if she was caught, she could be shot on the spot. Maybe sent to a camp she'd never return from, like those poor people on the train that night she had been stopped at the level-crossing barrier.

But Edda didn't falter. She remembered how she had coped when the Germans stormed their house, searching for the British paratrooper. And she would cope now. She was needed. And she would do what was asked of her. However terrified she felt.

She skirted the edge of the forest, past a clearing where a giant American bomber lay charred and smouldering. This was the one she had seen fall out of the sky like a meteorite. It was being guarded by three young German soldiers who studied Edda as she walked past them.

Edda smiled at them and began to skip down the lane, trying to behave like she was an innocent child playing a character on a stage. Those performances seemed a lifetime ago to her now. But she needed the enemy to think that she was just an ordinary girl perhaps going to visit a friend, not someone who knew exactly where the pilot of the crashed plane was hiding and was heading to meet him with some food and drink and a change of clothes so that he could disguise himself as a farmer and escape.

On one of the lanes, she had to move out of the way to let a German troop truck go thundering past. No doubt they were searching for the airman too. But Edda knew they were going in the wrong direction.

She looked at the ground. She felt the eyes of the enemy on her. If only they knew what she was doing. What would they do? Follow her? Wait until she found the airman, then shoot both of them?

Edda felt yet another wave of fear, an agonising

twist of pain in her stomach, before she turned off the road at a rock she had been told to use as a marker and made her way into the woods. She glanced to her left and right. There was no one around.

After waiting for five minutes in silence, hidden, listening for the enemy, Edda scrambled through the trees. Breathless, trying not to crack fallen branches underfoot or rustle through bushes, she headed west for a few minutes.

A sudden burst of noise made her squat down, and she looked up to see a large dark bird flapping through the bare branches. Her heart hammered hard and fast. She felt sick but pushed on.

Edda smelled him first. A waft of cigarette smoke. But not sharp, unpleasant German tobacco. It smelled rich and dizzying. American cigarettes.

Edda stopped and scanned the woods, looking

among the branches and leaves for a shape out of
place. And then she saw him, squatting in his ripped
US Air Force uniform, a large jacket hanging off him,
his eyes wide. His hair was slicked back, and Edda
thought that he looked like a film star but a little
roughed up. One of those square-jawed, bright-eyed
American men she used to watch in movies
before the Nazis had forced cinemas to show only
German films.

He was pointing a pistol at her.

She was cross with him. He was putting her in
danger too.

"Put out your cigarette," she whispered in
English. "The Germans will smell it for miles. You
might as well be waving an American flag."

The airman narrowed his eyes. "Are you
serious?" he asked, his cigarette burning bright at
the tip as he took a long drag.

Edda held the bundle of clothes she was carrying out in front of herself and stared hard at the American.

"Very," she replied. "If they smell your cigarette, they'll know you're here. German cigarettes smell sour. Yours is different. It gives you away. They will smell it on the other side of the forest."

The airman nodded and stubbed it out.

"I'm sorry," he said.

"These clothes are for you," Edda told him.

The airman put the pistol at his side. "I'm sorry about the cigarette," he said again. "I didn't think."

Edda dropped the package of clothes, food and water. "Here."

The airman was young. Maybe nineteen years old. Nearly the same age as Ian. He had dark brown eyes and cuts on his face, which was also smeared with mud.

Edda noticed his hands were trembling and that he was staring at her in disbelief.

"You're just a kid," the airman said.

Edda felt like she should correct him and say she was nearly sixteen, but she remembered she was to tell him nothing about herself. She knew why. If he was caught, he'd be asked who helped him. Under torture, he could quite easily give her away. If he knew she could speak English and that she was fifteen, it would not take long for the Germans to find her.

She reminded herself of the strict instructions she'd been given for her mission and said what she had been told to say.

"Where's your parachute?" Edda asked. "I need to hide it."

"I buried it back there. It's hidden. Don't worry."

"Good."

"What now?" the airman asked.

"We have people in the village who will come to meet you tonight, take you to a safe house, then on to Spain. Then England. Change into the clothes I've given you, and I will dispose of your uniform."

"You're English?" he asked, wincing in pain as he started to remove his jacket.

"Stop asking me questions," Edda insisted. "You don't need to know anything about me. And look, are you injured? I need to know so I can report it to those who are going to help you."

The airman shook his head. "Just a strain. A few scratches. Nothing broken. I can walk. But how is it they have sent a girl to help me? Have you run out of men to fight the war?"

Edda felt another flash of anger, thinking of her two brothers, of Uncle Otto. This airman's questions were irritating.

"Yes," she snapped, turning back round. "We use girls now because they get on with the job and don't sit around gossiping."

The airman laughed, covering his mouth, then he winced again and listened in silence as Edda told him what he needed to do and when he needed to do it. After she had finished, he suddenly looked ashamed and held out the hunk of bread she'd given him.

"You have some?" he offered. "You look like you've not eaten in weeks."

"It's for you," Edda said, registering that he didn't look thin. She had forgotten that people could look healthy and well fed. "I have to go. Good luck."

And then, after sharing what she hoped looked like a kind smile, Edda left. She had been told to be quick, to pass the message on and give him the supplies, then leave. Nothing more.

"Thank you," he said quietly as she moved away from him.

Working her way back through the woods, Edda found a bank of purple flowers and, after she had concealed the airman's flying kit under a rock in the stream that ran south, she picked some of the flowers for her mother.

Back on the track by the stone marker, Edda sighed. She felt exhausted from the tension of that short conversation with the airman. And shocked at how frightened she had been. She breathed in, then out.

Now she could relax.

She'd done it. Done something good. Something important. She had helped the resistance again, and she felt suddenly elated as she began to walk briskly home along the lane.

"Halt!" a sharp voice called out.

Edda heard the click of a rifle.

She saw a German soldier. Tall but young.

Her heart stopped. Was this it? Was she about to be arrested? She had to work hard not to throw up, she felt so frightened.

"ID," the soldier demanded. He was trying to look fierce, but Edda could see in his eyes that he was ill at ease.

She showed her ID card.

Now another soldier arrived.

"What are you doing here?" the second German soldier asked. This one was older, shouting, aiming a rifle at her as he approached.

Edda had to struggle to keep her legs from collapsing. She breathed in deeply.

"Flowers," she spluttered.

"What?"

Edda and the two soldiers stared at each other

in silence. In the distance she could hear the drone of aircraft high above them and the crackle of gunfire from the city.

"For my mum." Edda broke the silence. "She's sick. They are for her bedside. She likes woodland flowers."

And then Edda had an idea. She held the flowers out towards the older soldier. Her hands were shaking. And she figured that was good. "But you can take them for your mother," Edda said. "Would she like some flowers?"

Edda saw the soldier's face change. His eyes. It was in his eyes. The sadness. Edda realised he really was young too. *He* looked like a child now. The mention of his mother had changed him.

He shook his head. "No. Thank you. My mother is in Cologne. I have not seen her for ... Please go on. Take the flowers to your mother. I apologise."

"Thank you," Edda said. "I hope you get to see your mother soon." She meant it.

"Thank you," the soldier said. "I hope so too."

Edda walked fast down the lane. She had more confidence now. She had a script, something to say if she met any more patrolling soldiers. But she made it home without seeing anyone else.

Her mother was waiting for her in the garden when she returned, wringing her hands together, pacing the lawn. Edda wondered if Mum had been waiting there since she set out.

"You're back," Mum said, then, "Did you have a nice ... walk?"

Mum knew. Edda was sure of that. Knew that Edda had just put her life at risk to help the resistance.

"I brought you these," Edda said, handing her mum the flowers.

SEVENTEEN

Edda had stopped dancing altogether now. There was simply not enough food to enable her to do anything more than walk into Velp to collect their meagre rations from the butcher and baker and greengrocer, then return home and lie in bed. Just like there were not enough candles for them to light the cellar for more than an hour in the evening, meaning she had stopped reading and stopped drawing too.

Edda was hungry. But not just a rumbling-tummy kind of hunger. This was a hunger that made it feel like every molecule in her body was crying out for something to eat.

That winter, the Netherlands was starving. Most of the food and fuel and anything useful had been taken to Germany on heavily guarded trains. Even though people foraged in the fields and woods, there was barely any food to be found. The Dutch were dying every day of disease and hunger.

For breakfast they had one slice of bread made from pea flour, and a cup of hot water. For lunch, nothing. For dinner, a watery potato and nettle broth. That was it.

And after every meal, Edda still felt faint with hunger.

Edda, her mum and aunt and opa slept always in the cellar now. With German V1 rockets flying over nightly towards London, they had decided there was no point in taking a risk. And it made sense to heat the single cellar room only, now that there was no coal and little wood – in the middle of the

coldest winter to be inflicted on the Netherlands in a generation.

They used a bucket as a toilet, and it was Edda's job to empty it.

One morning, early, well before sunrise, they heard footsteps in a room above. They knew it could be anyone. A soldier looting their house. A neighbour so desperate for food they would be willing to steal. Someone coming to see if there was any furniture to burn.

Opa stood to go upstairs. Tentative. Nervous.

"Just leave them to it," Mum said.

Opa shook his head. "No. I can reason with them," he said, walking wearily upstairs.

"You're not going up there on your own," Mum said, and joined him.

Edda closed her eyes tight as she listened to two male voices in the room above. Then footsteps.

What was happening?

Who was upstairs?

Was it the Germans?

Were they here for her? Had they found out about the airman she had helped, the newsletters she had delivered?

Questions. Why were there always so many questions?

And then Opa and Mum appeared back in the cellar, another man on the steps behind them obscured by shadow at first.

What had he come for? To take something? Someone?

But then Edda saw who it was. Alex. Her brother. And without hesitating, she flung herself at him and held him so tight he cried out in pain.

"You came back," she said.

"I heard you were struggling for food. I thought,

as it's still dark, we could go on one of our night walks."

Edda almost burst into tears. A night walk. How long had it been since they'd done that?

They went out immediately, Mum warning them that Alex had to be back in hiding by the time the sun rose in a couple of hours. The Germans must not see him. But for now it was pitch-black.

"Where are we going?" Edda asked.

"Do you remember that bank of tulips in old Mr and Mrs Müller's place near the woods between Arnhem and Velp?" Alex whispered. "We used to walk past it every spring. There were hundreds of flowers. Remember?"

"I do," she said.

Edda's brother handed her a trowel. He was carrying a shovel and two large hessian sacks.

"Let's go and dig up the bulbs. The Müllers were

dirty collaborators. They did a runner when the British dropped in September last year. Their house has been looted and most of the floorboards have been taken for firewood, but maybe no one else has remembered the tulip bulbs."

It took half an hour to walk across the fields to the edge of Arnhem. They passed the bodies of several cattle, somehow killed in the crossfire. Edda retched when the stench of the rotting carcasses found its way into her nostrils. Then on to the outskirts of the city. Everywhere she looked, there was damage. Trees had been stripped of all their branches so that they looked like telegraph poles. The roofs of some of the houses had great holes in them, bricks and tiles scattered across gardens and streets.

The Müller house had been broken into. Its windows smashed and, as Alex had said, there

were no floorboards to be seen inside. The wooden window frames had been torn away too.

When they found the tulip bank, they were excited to see it was undisturbed. Brother and sister got to work straight away, digging down, unearthing tulip bulbs in the dark. The work was hard, but after a little over an hour, they had enough tulip bulbs to fill one of the sacks. There were maybe a hundred in there. Edda could anticipate the smell of the bulbs frying in the pan like onions.

As they dug, Edda fired questions at her brother. She wanted to know how Alex thought the war was going. Did he know anything that could give her hope?

Her brother was trying to sound positive. "I know the Allies are just a few kilometres away," he said. "On the other side of the river. It's only a matter of time before we are liberated. You just need to hold on, Edda."

"But when they parachuted into Arnhem, it failed," Edda said. "The Germans are still here."

"But weaker every day," Alex assured her. "The Allied bombing is killing Germany. Cities like Cologne and Dresden are being devastated. They're starving there too."

"So then they'll take all our food," Edda snapped. "We'll starve before they do. We ..." Edda found she couldn't speak. She was too emotional.

She felt her brother's hand on her shoulder. "I won't let you starve. You or Mum. Aunt Miesje. Opa. I'll find ways."

"And what happens when you starve? What then? I'm sorry. I never ask Mum about this, and I need to talk to someone."

Now Alex had his arms round Edda. The hug was warm, and she wanted it to go on for ever. But she noticed the horizon to the east and pushed him away.

"It's getting light," she warned.

Alex scowled. "You're right. If the Nazis see me, I'm toast."

They scurried through the outskirts of Arnhem, round the backs of gardens and through fields and small woods.

Edda could hardly believe what she saw. The city really had been smashed to pieces, as her grandfather had told her. Where once there had been houses with windows and curtains, now there were only piles of dust and broken bricks. Even the paving stones and kerb stones were shattered, driven over by tanks or broken by shellfire. A once elegant city, devastated. Edda stopped and stared back in disbelief.

"Come on," Alex urged. "We don't want to get caught now."

They walked along the railway line, Edda

gathering pieces of coal that had fallen from recent steam trains passing through and half filling the second sack.

"Let me carry it," Alex said, already straining with his sack of tulip bulbs.

"No," Edda disagreed, and pushed on, hearing a rumbling or buzzing noise that was hard to identify. An engine? Was someone coming? It was light now. What if the Nazis saw Alex? They'd take him like they took Ian. The trauma of that memory came back like a punch to Edda's chest.

They were three hundred metres from their grandfather's house when it happened. The noise of the engine was louder now. Much louder. Like a train roaring at them. But it wasn't a train. Alex reacted first, squatting, dragging Edda down to the ground from where she looked up to see a British Spitfire scouring the streets.

"Let's get home," Alex said. "The Germans won't hang around to question us with that beauty patrolling above the village."

Out in the open, they made a dash up the lane for home just as a German troop truck sped past, too fast to see them as it tried to evade the British fighter plane.

Down came the Spitfire, its cannons crackling, aiming directly for the truck, which had slammed on its brakes ahead of Edda and Alex. German soldiers spilled out and dived for the ditches and bushes on either side of the road.

As bullets tore up the lane in front of them, Edda scrambled for the trees, falling to her knees and gasping for air as she checked that her brother was safe.

Then, as suddenly as it had come, the roaring of the Spitfire faded and they were left with the smell

of the disturbed earth and the sound of the German soldiers laughing, unharmed as they lay in the ditches waiting to see if the Spitfire would return.

Why were they laughing? Edda wondered at first. A pilot was trying to kill them. They'd only just got away in time. Did they think that was funny? Really?

But then Edda caught Alex's eye and they were laughing too, gasping for air as tears streamed down their faces. This was madness. They were laughing, and the Germans were laughing, so loud they were unaware Edda and her brother had been caught up in the chaos too. Laughing at the fact they'd nearly all been killed.

Edda knew that this was not the laughter of happy people but of people who were living on the edge. She reached out for Alex. He put his arms round her and hugged her, and she wished he could be with her every day and not in hiding, leaving her with the

constant worry about whether the Germans would capture him, or what they would do to her, to everyone.

But she knew Alex was in grave danger.

"Go," she told him. "Now. I'll walk home past the soldiers. Distract them. You go back to wherever it is you've been hiding."

Alex laughed quietly. "My brave little sister," he said. "Look how fearless you have become. I am so proud of you!"

Edda had barely a second to comprehend what her brother had said before she pushed him away, wondering when she would see him again. If she would see him again. Then she heaved the sack of tulips onto her back, having to abandon the coal, and walked in the direction of the German soldiers. She didn't feel brave at all, but what choice did she have other than to carry on?

EIGHTEEN

Later that day, the family fried some of tulip bulbs that Edda and Alex had gathered. They tasted like onions but without the sharp tang. Nice, but nothing like real food – not like bread or meat or eggs.

So Edda was pleased when her mum asked her to go into the village the next morning to queue with their ration vouchers.

Each family had strips of ration vouchers, like stamps. These vouchers would be handed in at the butcher, baker or grocer, allowing you to buy so much meat, so many eggs, bread, vegetables and fruit. To receive your rations, you had to queue. And you had to be early in the queue because the shops quickly ran out of supplies.

Edda was happy to queue. To enjoy the fresh air and the light out of the cellar. She had sensed that spring was coming. The first signs were there.

Daffodils.

Buds on the trees.

Birds flitting about searching for nesting materials.

It was also good to see even more Vs painted on walls. V for victory. That was what they were all waiting for, hoping for. And the Vs always reminded Edda of Ian. Sometimes she imagined he had secretly come back and scrawled them on the walls and posters just for her.

As Edda walked through the streets, it was hard not to also see how utterly different Velp looked now.

German troop trucks and tanks were parked

underneath trees. Soldiers stood around smoking their sour tobacco. Nothing like the smell of the American airman's cigarette, Edda thought, wondering where he was now. Had he made it back to England? Was he safe? And where was Anje now? Edda had heard nothing from her or about her since the day she'd been forced to leave Velp.

The only local people who were out and about were those as desperate as Edda to get food. Nobody wanted to share their streets with the Germans.

As she arrived in the village square, grey clouds loomed low over the buildings, and Edda saw a group of girls in a cluster, two German soldiers holding them at gunpoint.

What was going on?

Sensing danger, Edda turned sharply to run back home.

Then stopped. Paralysed.

There was a German soldier standing in her way.

Edda felt more stupid than afraid. It was a trap.

The soldier gestured with his gun that she should join the other girls. Edda had no choice but to comply.

As she walked towards the group, head down, Edda was furious with herself for being caught. She immediately thought of how Mum would feel when she didn't come home. How she'd worry, then panic when it became dark, and how she'd rush into the village and ask around until someone told her that her daughter had been taken, just like her son.

Edda choked back a sob. She couldn't bear the thought that she might not see her mother again. But worse, that her mother might not see her again. It would kill her.

How could Edda have let this happen?

She stared upwards into the grey clouds. It had begun to rain, and she and the other girls were

quickly becoming wet. They stood silently, all just staring sullenly at the ground. And in turn, their captors, the Germans, stood dumbly watching them.

Edda's mind did what it always did. Asked questions. Why did the Germans want girls now? To work in factories too? Or worse? She had heard stories. The Germans were capable of anything. They disgusted her.

Her fury building, Edda looked at the soldiers. At their faces. Into their eyes. And she realised that most of them were really not that much older than her. It was something she'd heard other villagers commenting on – how most of the German soldiers they now saw were either old men or boys. Were the young men all dead? she wondered.

One of the soldiers smiled at her as he shivered in his wet uniform. Edda almost smiled back, then looked away in disgust. That word again.

Disgust.

At herself for starting to feel sorry for him. He had reminded Edda of her brothers. It seemed this whole group – the boy soldiers and girl prisoners – were children playing out a crazy scene in an even more crazy storybook.

This war was madness.

After a few minutes of grim silence, apart from the occasional sob from one of the captives, an older soldier arrived. Edda saw the young soldiers straighten their backs and become more alert as soon as he was there. Now their faces looked hard. No more smiles. And Edda understood from watching this that these boys had no idea what to do, just like the girls they had captured. Without this older man to choreograph them, they were clueless.

The older soldier shouted some orders, then marched off again, leaving the boys to drop their

shoulders and look, once more, like confused children. And Edda suddenly remembered *The Nutcracker*. A ballet she'd seen with her mum. Soldiers like puppets. Hapless. Comical. These young Nazis were just like that.

Behind her, Edda noticed, was an alleyway between two houses. There was a bend fifty metres down where the alleyway split and you could go to five or six different homes or into a small wood. She'd been that way delivering *De Oranjekrant*. She knew it well.

And with no time to think if she should do it, she ran.

Despite her hunger and weakness, Edda ran hard. All she needed to do was reach the bend in the alley, then the soldiers with their guns would not be able to shoot her.

Within seconds, she had twenty metres on

them, thirty, forty, fifty. And all the time she expected to hear a gunshot. A shout. But there was nothing.

Reaching the corner in the alley, she was tempted to look back but didn't. She would run and run and run until she knew she was safe. Then she would worry about her exhaustion, her weakness. About whether or not she was about to feel a bullet thump into the back of her head.

Once she was away from immediate danger and running through woods and then back gardens, Edda felt sick. She was worried about how her mum would react if she told her about nearly being rounded up. What if she didn't tell her? Then Mum wouldn't worry. Could she do that?

When she walked across the garden, Edda saw her mum watching through the back window. Waiting for her.

"What happened?" Mum came out, a towel in her hands. "Why are you home so soon? Why is your bag empty?"

Edda might have kept details about what she did for Dr Visser 't Hooft from her mother, but she would never lie to her.

"They're taking girls now," she confessed. "I was lucky. I managed to escape. But they had me for a minute."

Her mum let out the strangest noise. Like a sob or a cough. And then she was pulling at Edda, hurting her arm and shoulder.

"Inside," she shouted. "Inside now. The cellar. And you're not coming out again until we hear English voices on the streets."

Edda did as she was told. And she wondered if she'd ever see daylight again.

NINETEEN

Edda lay in the cellar, her bones pressing hard into the mattress she shared with her mum. She had been lying there for hours, or it could have been days. She couldn't really be sure about time passing now. Her hunger was so acute she could barely think.

But what she could do was listen. Lie there without using up any energy, eyes closed, making out the scream of a shell, the whipping sound of a bullet, the low buzz of a V1 rocket. She listened for footsteps too. Outside and in the house upstairs.

One night – only half-conscious – she had thought she heard a motorbike and dreamed that

Dr Visser 't Hooft had come to see her and placed his hand on her forehead. She dreamed he had said to Mum that Edda must rest now, that she had done her bit for the Netherlands, that their whole family had.

At least, she thought it was a dream.

She listened to the sound of her opa wheezing. Sometimes Aunt Miesje weeping. Mum snoring. All of them had become increasingly thin. Aunt Miesje's joints – like Edda's – had become swollen due to lack of food.

Somehow Mum had got hold of some vitamin tablets for them all. Edda wondered where she could have got them. Maybe Dr Visser 't Hooft *had* come that night? Maybe he had brought them on his motorbike? It was very hard to tell what was real and what was a dream. And Edda wasn't sure it mattered.

The days passed. It was spring outside. Edda

knew that. She wanted to go and sit in the garden and see the early spring flowers, sense the air. It smelled different in the spring – hopeful somehow.

But her mum had said she could only go upstairs first thing in the morning to wash, so, for most of the time, she could only imagine the smells and colours of spring from the grey cellar.

Sometimes she heard a train in the distance and she always wondered who was on it and where they were going, thinking about the people she had seen being taken from the station in Velp that first night she had delivered *De Oranjekrant*. And she thought how she could have been put on a train herself if she'd not got away from the young soldiers the last day she was in the village.

Those were the thoughts that stopped Edda feeling too hungry. Those and the stories her mum would tell her about the future. About how, when

the war was over and they were strong again, Mum would take her to all the great cities of the world. London. New York. Paris. And Edda would go to dance school, would join a ballet company and become one of the most famous dancers the world had ever seen.

As she dozed, Mum would fill her with dreams of glitter and glamour. And for a while, those dreams would sustain Edda and stop her thinking about food and the pains cramping through her body.

When her hunger was at its worst, making her double over and her mood dip, she sometimes imagined a V1 rocket stopping in the sky directly above their house, its engine failing, then plunging through the attics, the ceilings and floors and into the cellar. It would be quick, simple. Sometimes she couldn't help thinking that at least if that happened she wouldn't feel hungry any more.

And then one evening, after the sun had

gone down and a wintery cold returned with the darkness, there was a knock at the door.

It was late. Well past the curfew hour.

As was customary when there was a knock at the door or the sound of someone in the house above them, the four inhabitants of the cellar looked at each other, trying to work out what to do without speaking.

Mum instinctively slid next to Edda and hugged her, but it hurt. Now that Edda had lost so much more weight, even a touch from her mother felt painful. She had no flesh on her to protect her bones. Her elbows ached too. They were swollen like her knees.

"I don't know what to do," Opa finally said in response to the knock at the door.

No one replied. They were in shock. Opa – the head of the family – didn't know what to do. This

man who had always been in charge, a man of
authority who made them feel safe, said he didn't
know what to do. His admission was hard to take.

Another knock.

Was this it? Edda wondered. The Germans come
to take them away? Had they found out about the
airman, the dark evenings, something? Or about
Opa listening to the radio? Would this be the day
they were taken from their home and put on a
train? Edda and her family had done enough for the
resistance to warrant such punishment.

She closed her eyes and fell back on the mattress.

"Should we leave it? Pretend we're not here?"
Opa asked.

"I'll go," Mum said, shaking her head. "They
might come in. Loot. We don't know. It's better to
face them."

Opa followed Mum up the stairs. Edda could

hear them talking after they had opened the door. Then silence. Next she heard her mother bursting into tears. In the dark, every word, every tone of voice, every laugh or sob meant more than ever. What was going on?

Edda struggled to stand up to see her mother coming into the room. Was she crying or laughing? It was impossible to tell. And, anyway, people laughed when they were scared these days, cried when they were happy. The war had turned everything on its head.

So what was it now?

Was Alex dead?

Was Ian home?

Was the war over?

What had changed?

Edda just wanted to know. However bad the news was, she wanted to hear it.

Then she saw that Opa had appeared and that he was carrying a box. There were words on the side in another language.

"Food," Opa said, seeing Edda's face, his voice faltering. "From someone. We couldn't see who it was though. We called after them, but they had already gone. But I had heard ... I had heard that the British and the Americans have been dropping food parcels."

They all stared with awe into the open box. At tins marked "Stew" in English. "Whole Milk Powder". And three packs marked "US Army Field Ration No. 2". Tins of food and jars of preserved fruit. And two blankets. It was a miracle.

Her ears still attuned to the night, Edda heard the distinct sound of a motorbike engine starting up then fading.

And then they ate.

TWENTY

The war raged on in the world above Edda's damp cellar. Night after night of gunfire and mortar shells, with the fighting coming closer. Outside, the village was in pieces. The few times Edda managed to take a peek at the streets and buildings she had known so well, she saw devastation. It felt to her like there wasn't much more that could be destroyed. Just the people hiding in their cellars waiting for the war to finish – or to finish them off.

Edda no longer jumped at the noises – there was nothing she could do to stop them. And it wasn't the sounds of war that troubled her most anyway.

It was her hunger.

Even with the food parcel from the resistance –
and others that had been airdropped by British
Lancaster bombers flying so low she'd heard you
could see the pilots waving – Edda was dangerously
underfed. She had to lie on her side, as she could feel
the bones of her back and backside pressing into
the mattress if she lay on her back. She felt terribly
weak, and her stomach craved food. And she knew
that this could only go on for so long. If Edda didn't
get some more food to eat, it was very possible that
she would starve to death.

Hundreds of people were dying for lack of food
in the Netherlands every day. Edda had read this in
copies of *De Oranjekrant*. Would she become one of
those? A body lying dead? She remembered again
what Anje had said about seeing a corpse. It had
stuck with her. The idea that she might end up like

that too. Not on a road covered in dust, but in a cellar, a blanket over her.

Edda tried to distract herself during the night by choreographing imaginary dancing. Practising in her head what she couldn't do on stage or at the barre now. But even thinking about dancing was exhausting after a while, and her mind drifted.

Eventually it was morning again. The best part of her day.

Edda would go to wash in the kitchen sink and check all was well in the house. This was the only time she was allowed out of the cellar, allowed to use up energy. Her mum had said it was safe so early, before anyone else was about. Edda lived for these moments.

It was now mid April. The air smelled sweeter, and the mornings were lighter. In the garden, flowers were blooming around the edges of the lawn,

though fewer than usual as most of the bulbs had been dug up and eaten.

Easing the door open to enjoy the spring morning, Edda smelled something different as she squinted in the bright sunlight. A sweet aroma. But not flowers. No. Not flowers.

Edda gasped. It couldn't be.

She inhaled again. And listened more attentively than ever. It was quiet. Really quiet.

The hairs on Edda's arm went up.

She knew. Instinctively she knew. It was over.

Edda felt a sob come up from her chest.

Her eyes widened as a group of soldiers appeared round the side of the house. She stepped backwards, ready to shut the door and hide.

And then she saw that the soldiers were not dressed in grey. But in beige. And they were walking towards her. Smiling.

"Mum. Opa!" Edda shouted at the top of her voice. "Aunt Miesje. Come now. Come and see!"

The soldiers approached carefully, smiling still. They looked well fed, like the American airman had. Not like the gaunt, ever-thinner faces of her family that Edda had to look at every day in the cellar.

There was a polar bear design on the arm of one of the men. Edda remembered Ian telling her that Canadians wore a polar bear on their shoulders.

"Hey, miss!" the soldier called out. "Do you speak English?"

Edda stepped out onto the patio at the back of the house. "Yes. We all do. I'm English, sort of."

"Well, I'm Canadian, and it's a pleasure to hear the voice of an English girl after all we've been through."

Mum and Opa and Aunt Miesje were now behind Edda in the doorway. Silent. Wary.

"Good morning, ladies. Sir," the Canadian soldier said, "I am pleased to inform you that you have been liberated. Got any Germans hiding away anywhere?"

Liberated!

Edda gasped, then ran and threw her arms round the soldier, followed quickly by her mother and aunt and a vigorous handshake from Opa.

The soldier grinned and pointed to the main road where children were running with orange flags trailing behind them. Edda could now hear the sounds of cheering and laughing.

Liberated!

And now she saw not just the neighbours she knew so well but many more people. Men and women coming out of hiding. *Onderduikers*. Former neighbours whom she thought had left or died. And trucks filled with Canadian and British soldiers.

More children waving small Dutch flags attached to sticks. It was like a carnival.

Edda felt an arm on her shoulder and turned to smile at her mum.

"Liberated," Mum said, struggling to get the word out.

Edda grinned through her tears. She realised she was crying. She couldn't believe this was happening.

The war was over. They would have food. They would see Alex and Ian. This was it. The day they had all dreamed of.

Edda burst into tears again and hugged her mother hard. Then she noticed a car edging slowly up the road from the centre of the village, people parting to let it through.

She felt her mum's body go rigid.

"What is it?" Edda asked.

"I'm not sure, my love," Mum said. And they watched as the car approached with a man attached to the front, tied with rope, wearing what looked like his nightclothes.

The scene was horrible. And Edda couldn't understand why people were cheering and shouting.

"Sympathiser!" a voice screamed in rage.

"Collaborator!" said another.

"They're coming for the sympathisers," Mum said quietly, her eyes on Edda's. "Those not to be trusted. You understand?"

Edda nodded. Her chest had tightened.

The phrase Mum had used sent a chill through her body. *Those not to be trusted.* Then an army vehicle was coming towards them, carrying two men wearing orange armbands and a Canadian army officer.

A silence fell over the part of the crowd where

the vehicle stopped. The men climbed out and walked towards Edda and her family.

Mum's hand was on Edda's shoulder again. "I think they're here for me," she whispered to Edda as Opa moved to stand in front of her. He looked so small and frightened.

"Ella van Heemstra?" the Canadian soldier asked.

"Yes. That is me," Mum said, head held high.

"Please would you come with us?"

Mum stepped towards the soldier, her hand slipping out of Edda's after a brief squeeze.

And then she was taken. Led to the vehicle. Eased inside. And Edda fell to her knees.

TWENTY-ONE

Edda watched Mum, inside the vehicle now. She was mouthing something through the glass before the engine revved and she was carried away down the lane, dust kicking up behind the tyres.

Was this how the war would end for them? Not with orange flags and dancing in the streets but with Mum being arrested? Edda stared into her opa's eyes. Then Aunt Miesje's eyes.

They said nothing.

They did nothing.

But Edda *would* do something. She was not going to wait to see how things played out. How had they played out with Uncle Otto? With Ian? With Alex? She needed to act, to change things.

The hospital. She would go to the hospital. She would find Dr Visser 't Hooft and demand that he do something to help Mum.

So now she was running. Her legs like jelly, breaths sharp and painful. She was still so weak from hunger.

As she ran from her home to the hospital, she went over all the things she had done to prove that her family were to be trusted.

Delivering newsletters. Dancing to raise money. Assisting downed airmen.

And the things Mum had done too.

Helping Edda to dance at the dark evenings. Hiding the paratrooper in her own home. Looking after the refugees from Arnhem. Allowing Edda to do all the things she had done to help Dr Visser 't Hooft.

Had the resistance forgotten all that because Mum had, at one point, many years ago, admired Hitler? They needed to know that she had understood her errors and done a hundred things to help the resistance since.

Edda's anger caused her to run faster, tapping into strength she didn't know she had. She was at the hospital door in minutes. To find more people waving orange flags. More people dancing in circles. More smiling and laughing.

And then she saw him. Dr Visser 't Hooft. He was already looking at her, his own smile fading from his face. Could the doctor see that Edda was the only one not happy, not waving orange around?

He ran to her. "What is it, Edda?"

Now she had to put into words her latest trauma, Edda felt a wave of emotion. It was so powerful that she couldn't speak for a moment.

"Edda?" Dr Visser 't Hooft asked again.

"They have Mum," Edda gasped. "The resistance. The Canadians. They've taken her to the village hall. I need you to—"

The doctor grabbed Edda's hand. "Come on," he said.

And they ran. Ran to his motorcycle, which was leaning against the side of the hospital building. He climbed onto it, fired the engine, then turned to Edda.

"Get on. And hold on."

They sped quickly through the crowds, Edda with her arms wrapped round the doctor as warm air rippled around her, the tide of people dancing in the streets parting at the familiar roar of the doctor's motorbike.

Left down Tramstraat. Right along the main road. Then fast to the village hall, where Edda saw

what she thought was the vehicle that had taken Mum.

"There," she said, releasing the doctor, who braked hard and climbed off the motorcycle, then began to run towards the building.

"Wait here," he said, looking back.

There was a larger crowd celebrating in the centre of Velp. Bottles being passed round under flashes of orange material. A scarf. A flag. A handkerchief. Everyone seemed to be wearing something orange, declaring their devotion to the resistance. Allied soldiers being hugged and kissed. Dancing in circles.

Edda swore she would never dance again if anything happened to Mum. Dance was nothing to her without her mum.

Now, as she waited for the doctor to do something to help, Edda saw two women on their knees in front of the village hall, sobbing as they were goaded by a mob. They had had their hair shaved. Edda studied them for a few seconds. These women had been friendly with the occupiers. This was their punishment. And everyone was enjoying watching them suffer.

Edda wondered if this might happen to her mum. Was she about to be brought out of the village hall, her hair shaved, put on her knees for the whole of the village to abuse?

Surely not.

A man came to stand beside her. Edda didn't recognise him at first. He was wearing a jacket. Alex. He looked smart. Like Alex from years ago, Alex before the war.

"They've got Mum," her brother croaked. "Where's Visser 't Hooft?"

"In there," Edda said. She felt sick. Sick and angry.

Alex smiled at Edda. "Then she will be OK," he said.

"Will she?"

"She will," Alex said. "I have no idea what you've done, but whatever it is, Dr Visser 't Hooft thinks the world of you, Audrey."

Edda shrugged, ignoring the fact he'd used her real name and what that meant. That the war was over now. That they didn't need to pretend. She didn't want to believe that all was going to be well until it was. Didn't dare hope.

They waited, eyeing the heavy wooden door of the village hall, joined soon by Opa and Aunt Miesje.

*

Time passed.

Exhausted now, Edda sat on a broken kerb that had been smashed by a shell and held her head in her hands. And although her brother and aunt and opa tried to comfort her, there was nothing they could say. Because no one understood Edda like her mum. No one.

Edda thought about the future she and her mum had talked about. What they would do after the war. Edda would dance all over Europe. The world. And her mum would come with her, finding work wherever Edda danced. Edda had never dared to really hope for that, to invest in it, so fearful it would never happen. She was even more afraid now. She buried her hopes and dismissed her future.

Time seemed to slow until – eventually – the door to the village hall creaked slowly open. And there stood Mum.

Her hair was intact. Her clothes were neat as usual as she scanned the crowd.

Edda ran at her. Fast and hard. Mother and daughter fell into each other's arms.

TWENTY-TWO

Even though Mum had been released and Alex could come and go as he pleased, and even though they were allowed out of their house whenever they liked and they were able to tear the blackout frames off their windows, Edda and her family were still on edge.

Like so many other families, there was someone unaccounted for at home.

For Edda's family, it was Ian.

The word was that those who had been working as *Arbeitseinsatz* in Germany were coming home now. The Red Cross had fed them and in some cases

offered to transport them to the towns and villages from where they had been brutally abducted. Word also came, however, that some of the young men taken would not be coming back. They had been killed trying to escape the Nazis. They had, in some cases, starved to death.

There was no word of Ian either way.

Over the next few days, Mum would try to distract Edda by sitting with her on the front porch, talking through their plans of joining a dance school, moving to Amsterdam or London. Becoming a famous dancer.

But Edda couldn't cope with those conversations. She would just watch people coming up the road. Always with an eye out for men on their own. That was what it would be like, she imagined. She would see a lone figure walking, then breaking into a run, calling out. She imagined it over and over as she stared between trees now heavy with blossom.

But three, four, then five days passed and Ian did not come home, and Edda began to fear the worst.

And then, one day, while Edda was repairing her bicycle, happy to be able to use it again now the Germans had gone, she saw a figure walking up the street from the centre of the village.

"It's Ian," Edda said to Mum. She stood, her heart hammering.

Mum peered down the road. "You can't tell from here."

Edda shook her head. Mum was wrong.

She walked down the steps of the front porch, then across the front garden and stared down the road. Edda put her hand to her eyes to shield them from the sun, and she watched until the figure raised two fingers, making the V sign.

V for victory.

Vrijheid.

Freedom.

9-23

AUDREY HEPBURN

WHY AUDREY HEPBURN?

Resist is the story of Edda and her family's experiences in
the occupied Netherlands during the Second World War.
It was inspired by the true story of the teenage years of
one of the most iconic Hollywood film stars of all time,
Audrey Hepburn.

Audrey Hepburn is best known for her roles in films
like *Breakfast at Tiffany's* and *My Fair Lady*, and also as a
tireless campaigner for children's rights through UNICEF,
the United Nations Children's Fund. But it was the story of
her childhood that inspired me to write this book.

Audrey did not speak a great deal about her
childhood – about what happened to her during the war
and what happened to her family. But some of the things
she did say in various interviews during her life, along with
the work of biographers and film-makers, has given us a
little insight into those years. This book is a work of fiction
inspired by these insights.

It is not a biography. But the story has been intensely

and – I hope – sensitively researched, and it is as close as I could get to what I think a young Audrey Hepburn would have been like. It is based both on what those who knew her have said about her and the stories of other children who lived in the Netherlands during the occupation, such as Anne Frank, Anje van Maanen and Sid Baron, among others.

*

Audrey was born in Belgium in 1929 to a Dutch mother and British father, who separated when she was six. She was at boarding school in England when the Second World War broke out in 1939, and her parents decided she would be safer in the Netherlands with her mother, opa (grandfather) and brothers, Alex and Ian.

So in 1940, just before the Germans invaded the Netherlands, Audrey flew back from England to live first in Arnhem, then nearby Velp. After the occupation, Audrey's mother decided to have her use the name "Edda", as "Audrey" was obviously British and she was worried that it would draw the enemy's attention.

From the interviews and biographies mentioned above, I learned that she delivered resistance newsletters.

That her uncle was murdered, her brothers enslaved and forced into hiding. She talked about helping downed airmen and dancing at illegal events to raise money to help the resistance – acts that she would have done knowing that she and her family would be made to suffer gravely if she was caught by the enemy.

It is a story so remarkable that I could not resist trying to reimagine it for children today.

Audrey Hepburn and her mother, Ella van Heemstra.

OCCUPATION AND STARVATION

The Netherlands was just one of numerous European countries invaded and occupied by the Germans during the Second World War.

Many were invaded as part of Hitler's plan called *Lebensraum*, which means "living space". Hitler believed Germany needed more space in order to survive and be a successful nation in the future, and that the only way to achieve this was to expand eastwards. Other occupied countries were invaded for strategic reasons and to gain vital war resources.

The Netherlands was invaded on 10 May 1940 as part of the German plan to reach and conquer France. The whole country was soon under German control. Many people were forced from their homes and many were forced to work to support the German war effort.

In *Resist* we see Edda's brother Ian being captured by the Nazis for *Arbeitseinsatz*, which was a policy forcing every man aged between eighteen and forty-five to work

in German factories. Around half a million men were transported to Germany as a result and forced to work under terrible conditions doing hard labour.

The Jewish population of the Netherlands was persecuted by the Nazis during the occupation, as they were across Europe, and from 1941, Dutch Jews were rounded up and transported to concentration camps, as Edda witnessed. Of the 140,000 Jews living in the Netherlands in 1940, only around 38,000 had survived by the time the war ended in 1945.

Towards the end of *Resist* we hear about the terrible hunger that Edda and her family endured in the winter of 1944–45, when Edda was so weak her mother was afraid that she might die. Throughout the occupation, the Nazis forced the Dutch population to supply them with food – some historians estimate that 60 per cent of the food produced in the Netherlands from 1940 to 1944 was exported by the Germans. But in the winter of 1944 things got much worse.

There was a Dutch railway strike, which was intended to help the Allies and hinder the Nazis. But the Germans hit back by stopping food deliveries to western parts of the country. That year there was also a very hard winter and a poor harvest due to the destruction and flooding of

agricultural land, and all of these factors meant that food stocks quickly ran out. It is estimated that 22,000 died as a result of this famine, or *Hongerwinter* as it was called in Dutch, and it only ended with the liberation of the country in 1945.

RESISTANCE

After the Nazis invaded and occupied countries throughout Europe, various secret groups were formed to oppose them. It's not known how many people took part or who they all were. But we do know that many ordinary people were involved, as well as some armed fighters. We know them now as the resistance, but they took different forms in different countries.

In the Netherlands the resistance was organised by people who were outraged about the invasion of their country and then outraged about the way the Jewish population was being treated by the invaders. They formed small independent groups and carried out activities intended to disrupt Nazi plans. They helped Jewish people to escape and also provided shelter for those who needed to hide. They forged ration cards and money, and provided the Allies with a lot of useful information that they could use to fight back against the Nazis. They also sabotaged phone lines and railways. Resistance members who were caught were usually immediately sentenced to death.

ANNE FRANK AND AUDREY HEPBURN

Audrey Hepburn lived in the Netherlands at the same time that Anne Frank was writing her famous diary, which told the story of Anne's family living in a secret annex in Amsterdam to avoid being found by the Nazi occupiers.

Whilst Audrey was working for the resistance to help defeat the Nazis, Anne Frank was forced to hide. This was because Anne and her family were Jewish and the Nazis planned to capture and murder all Jews in Europe.

Although she nearly starved to death, Audrey survived the war and went on to have a fabulous career, but she would always be aware of Anne Frank and her important legacy.

Two years after the war – while living in Amsterdam with her mother – Audrey was shown the manuscript of Anne Frank's diary before it was published. Reading it had a huge effect on her. The diary echoed some of the experiences she had had herself in the occupied Netherlands.

Their lives were very different, of course, but they did have some things in common, having lived in the same country through the same period of history and being the same age. Audrey read about the first five death candidates being executed in Anne's diary, knowing that Anne was speaking about her own beloved uncle, Otto.

Anne Frank's father, also called Otto, survived the Holocaust. He went on to publish his daughter's diary so that people would remember her story. After the war, he asked Audrey – who was by now a very famous actor – if she would play Anne in the film of the book. Audrey declined, worried that it would bring back many traumatic memories and would not be good for her. In later years, she did read from the diary on film to raise money for UNICEF.

To find out about the work done by the Anne Frank Trust to fight prejudice and discrimination in the UK, please visit **www.annefrank.org.uk**.

AUDREY HEPBURN AND UNICEF

"I can testify to what UNICEF means to children, because I was among those who received food and medical relief after World War II. I have a long-lasting gratitude and trust for what UNICEF does."
– AUDREY HEPBURN

Driven by the memories of what she suffered during the Second World War, Audrey Hepburn was committed throughout the rest of her life to fighting for children's rights across the world.

In 1989 she became a UNICEF goodwill ambassador. UNICEF works to help improve the lives of children all around the world, especially when there is a crisis like a war or a famine, both of which Audrey knew all too much about.

Audrey travelled to countries including Ethiopia, Guatemala and the Sudan to meet those helping children

and to raise awareness of their work by giving countless interviews to the media. She also spoke to politicians around the world to try to persuade them to do more to help children.

She gave up being an actor to focus on helping UNICEF and children, and continued her work even when she was very ill. She died in 1993 at the age of 63.

Find out more about UNICEF and their work or donate to support them at **www.unicef.org.uk**.

RESEARCH

I always do a lot of research to try my hardest not to misrepresent history and real people's lives. My research includes visiting museums, watching films, reading books and much more. This is a summary of the tip of the iceberg of my research.

Amsterdam has an amazing array of museums. The museums in the city's Jewish Quarter are brilliant, educational and thought-provoking, as are the Anne Frank Haus and the Resistance Museum – the Verzetsmuseum – where I learned huge amounts about the occupation of the Netherlands during the Second World War.

The best history book I read was *A Street in Arnhem* by Robert Kershaw. This was a huge help – along with Anje van Maanen's extraordinary diary of being a child in Arnhem during the war.

The best biographies of Audrey Hepburn are *Audrey Hepburn* by Barry Paris, *Audrey Hepburn: Fair Lady of the*

Screen by Ian Woodward and *Dutch Girl: Audrey Hepburn and World War II* by Robert Matzen.

Children's books that I'd recommend about the same period of history and set in the Netherlands are *Tamar* by Mal Peet, *Winter in Wartime* by Jan Terlouw and *The Diary of a Young Girl* by Anne Frank.

Books for adults that helped included *The Hiding Place* by Corrie Ten Boom, *The Cut Out Girl* by Bart van Es, Sean Hepburn Ferrer's *Audrey Hepburn, An Elegant Spirit*, Sid Baron's *The Way it Was*, *My Name Is Selma* by Selma van de Perre and *The Assault* by Harry Mulisch.

I'd also recommend the two biopics of Audrey Hepburn: one by Helena Coan called *Audrey*; the other is *Looking for Audrey Hepburn* by Darcey Bussell.

ACKNOWLEDGEMENTS

This book is dedicated to Ailsa Bathgate, my editor at Barrington Stoke. Ailsa has edited my books *Armistice Runner*, *D-Day Dog*, *After the War*, *Arctic Star* and now this one. As a result of how Ailsa has challenged and nurtured me, my career has not just continued but thrived. That's down to Ailsa, and I feel blessed to have her as an editor.

Huge thanks, as always, to my regular first readers, Rebecca Palmer and Simon Robinson.

Thank you also – for helping me with Dutch history – to Caroline Bennett (the International School, Groningen), Rachel Stephenson and Lorraine (the British School in the Netherlands), Abi Byrne (the British School of Amsterdam) and Carla Hubertson. Also Helen McCord from UCL London.

I'd also like to thank the girls and teachers of Channing School in London who read the book and gave me some great feedback. Thank you also to Jane Broadis for her excellent feedback.

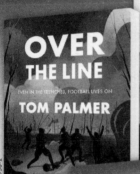

OVER
THE LINE
EVEN IN THE TRENCHES, FOOTBALL LIVES ON
TOM PALMER

978-1-78112-956-2

AFTER
THE WAR
FROM AUSCHWITZ TO AMBLESIDE
TOM PALMER

978-1-78112-948-7

ARCTIC
STAR
BRAVING THE WORST JOURNEY IN THE WORLD
TOM PALMER

978-1-78112-971-5

ARMISTICE
RUNNER
TWO LIVES CONNECTED BY MEMORY
TOM PALMER

978-1-78112-825-1

D-DAY
DOG
TOM PALMER

978-1-78112-868-8

Barrington Stoke